THE RO
and other Boer

Herman Charles Bosman

THE ROOINEK
and other Boer War stories

Edited by Craig MacKenzie

Human & Rousseau
Cape Town Pretoria Johannesburg

Herman Charles Bosman was born in Kuils River near Cape Town in 1905, but spent most of his life in the Transvaal. In 1926 he was posted as a young teacher to a farm school near Zwingli in the Marico District of what was then the Western Transvaal. This position was abruptly terminated after he was arrested and convicted for the murder of his stepbrother during a vacation at the family home in Johannesburg. He spent four years in gaol after his death sentence was commuted to life imprisonment.

After his release on parole in 1930 he worked as a journalist in Johannesburg before leaving for London in 1934, where he was to spend the next six years. Returning to South Africa in 1940, he resumed his career as a journalist and editor until his sudden death from heart failure in 1951. In his lifetime he saw only three of his works into print: *Jacaranda in the Night* (1947), *Mafeking Road* (1947) and *Cold Stone Jug* (1949), his prison memoir.

The stories gathered here were written between 1931 (shortly after his release from prison) and 1951, the year of his death. Some were published only posthumously. The Boer War was therefore a theme to which he returned sporadically throughout his life, his interest having initially been sparked by war stories he heard from farmers in the Marico District.

CONTENTS

INTRODUCTION

Herman Charles Bosman (1905–1951) was born less than three years after the end of what is now known as the Anglo–Boer South African War, and yet it is in some ways fortuitous that this momentous event in South African history came to feature in his work at all. As the first story in this collection reveals, in January, 1926, at the whim of the Transvaal Education Department, he was sent as a novice teacher to a farm school in the Dwarsberg area of the Groot Marico. His activities as a teacher included 'huisbesoek' – house visits to the parents of the children in his school. In this way he discovered that the community contained several skilful storytellers whose tales of the past would invariably include memorable ones dealing with the Boer War.

Bosman's sojourn in the Marico was cut short when he was convicted for shooting and killing his stepbrother at the family home in Johannesburg during the July school vacation. A painful interlude in prison followed, but when in the early 1930s he turned to writing in earnest, it was to the Marico region that he famously returned in the form of some 150 'Bushveld' stories.

Typically, he was drawn to tales about the war dealing with the quirky, less admirable aspects of human nature – cowardice, duplicity, vainglory – and it is these failings that he gently but incisively reveals to lie beneath the glossy patina of Boer mythology. He was, after all, pre-eminently a satirist, and the glamorous, embellished tales that he encountered in the Bushveld clearly aroused his sharpest debunking instincts. Despite this, the characters that one encounters in these tales are sympathetically drawn. In all of us, Bosman appears to be saying, lies the potential for both nobility and ignominy; it all depends on circumstance. As one of the characters in "The Red Coat" puts it, "if, at the battle of Bronkhorstspruit, Piet Niemand did perhaps run at one stage, it was the sort of thing that could happen to any man; and for which any man could be forgiven, too."

The stories in this volume have been arranged in a deliberate sequence. The first, "The Affair at Ysterspruit", sets the scene. It uses an authorial narrator and provides insights into how it was that Bosman as a young teacher came to encounter tales about the two Anglo–Boer Wars. This and the last story, "A Boer Rip van Winkel" (which also uses an authorial narrator), together provide a contextualising frame for the intervening nine stories, all of which are 'Oom Schalk Lourens' tales.

The second and third stories, "Yellow Moepels" and "The Red Coat", deal with the First Anglo–Boer War of 1880–81, while the fourth story, "Funeral Earth", tellingly links the skirmishes between the Boers and various African tribes of the last decades of the nineteenth century to the looming cataclysm of 1899–1902. The five stories that then follow deal squarely with the Second Anglo–Boer War and are arranged roughly chronologically. One moves, in other words, through some of the key progressions of the war – from the large-scale engagements in Natal, through defeat at Mafeking, to headlong retreat to the Eastern Transvaal, and finally to the inconclusive, sporadic warfare of the 'small commandos'. The penultimate story, "The Rooinek", deals mainly with the aftermath of the war, while the last, "A Boer Rip van Winkel", links the war to the 1914 Rebellion. Some thirty-five years of conflict are thus represented here with the 1899–1902 hostilities as their climactic centrepiece.

The stories were written between 1931 and 1951 (the year of Bosman's death). The Boer War was thus a topic to which he returned throughout his active writing life, although it never became a dominant theme, *pace* a critic's remark (in a review of the posthumously published *Unto Dust* in the *Times Literary Supplement* of 15 March, 1963) that Bosman made "a reputation for himself by telling old tales of the Boer War." This impression was no doubt engendered by the fact that some of Bosman's most finely wrought stories – "The Rooinek", "Mafeking Road", and "Funeral Earth" among them – deal with the war.

References to the two Anglo–Boer Wars also occur in other stories, perhaps most famously (and hilariously) in "In the Withaak's Shade", in which Oom Schalk describes the fever of activity occasioned by the discovery of a leopard in the neighbourhood: "Exciting times followed.

There was a great deal of shooting at the leopard and a great deal of running away from him. The amount of Martini and Mauser fire I heard in the krantzes reminded me of nothing so much as the First Boer War. And the amount of running away reminded me of nothing so much as the Second Boer War." It is noteworthy that even in this brief reference, casually interpolated into a story that has nothing to do with the war, Bosman's satirical intention is clear.

Bosman's relationship to his own Afrikaner heritage is thus ambiguous. He may say (through the voice of his narrator in "The Affair at Ysterspruit") that, when shown a photograph of a veteran of the war, "it was always with a thrill of pride in my land and my people that I looked on a likeness of a hero of the Boer War." However, in his fictional portrayals of the events of the two wars (Sir Theophilus Shepstone's annexation of the Transvaal in 1877, the battle of Bronkhorstspruit in 1879 and of Majuba Hill in 1881; the siege of Mafeking in the Second Anglo–Boer War, the defeat of Louis Botha at Dalmanutha and the later skirmishes of the 'small commandos') it is the telling human weakness that he lifts out of the surrounding swath of historical data. This is Bosman's Boer War – a war in which heroism is never free from the element of self-doubt, in which self-interest frequently asserts itself in moments of crisis, in which resolve falters under the hail of English lyddite and the shabby remnants of once mighty commandos roam disconsolately over the desolate veld. . .

Somewhat paradoxically, though, what ultimately emerges from this piecemeal portrait of the Boer War is a sense of the protagonists' inner nobility and irreducible human value. Like Oom Herklaas van Wyk in the concluding story, "A Boer Rip van Winkel", they seem to emanate "a strange kind of assurance, a form of steadfastness in the face of adversity and defeat." It is Bosman's singular achievement – having already stripped away all of the comforting layers of bravado and self-deception – to leave the reader with this poignant after-effect.

Craig MacKenzie
Johannesburg, 2000

11

Illustrations accompanying the original publications of some of the stories

The *Touleier*, January-February, 1931; artist: A. E. Mason

"She stood with the early wind of winter ruffling her skirts, and watched the commando riding by." (*Spotlight*, February, 1951; artist: 'Flip')

"We saw him riding out under the starlight, following after his son and shouting to him to be a man and to fight for his country." ("The Mafeking Road"; *South African Opinion*, 23 August, 1935; artist: 'R.L.')

"Mafeking Road"; *South African Opinion*, December 1944; artist: Donald Harris

NOTES ON THE TEXT

In editing this collection reliable copy-texts have been used. The stories in many cases appeared in several editions over the years and errors were inevitably introduced. I have therefore returned to the first published versions, some of which appeared in periodicals that were under Bosman's own editorial scrutiny. Where stories were republished by Bosman, I have followed these later versions. In several cases – notably "The Traitor's Wife", "The Red Coat", "The Question" and "A Boer Rip van Winkel" – manuscripts held at the Harry Ransom Humanities Research Center in Texas were consulted.

1. "The Rooinek" (Parts 1 and 2). *Touleier* 1.2 (Jan–Feb 1931): 8–13 and 1.3 (Mar 1931): 126–132.

2. "Karel Flysman." *The African Magazine* 1.1 (June 1931): 379–381.

3. "Yellow Moepels." *South African Opinion* 1.7 (25 Jan 1935): 7–8; reprinted *South African Opinion* 2.2 (Apr 1945): 14–15.

4. "The Mafeking Road." *South African Opinion* 1.22 (23 Aug 1935): 6–7; reprinted as "Mafeking Road", *South African Opinion* 1.10 (Dec 1944): 12–13, 28.

5. "Die Voorval by Ijzerspruit." *Die Ruiter* 1.48 (2 Apr 1948): 7, 43; in English as "The Affair at Ysterspruit." *Unto Dust*: 121–126.

6. "Funeral Earth." *Vista* (1950): 62–65.

7. "Peaches Ripening in the Sun." *On Parade* 3.5 (27 Feb 1951): 12–13.

8. "The Traitor's Wife." *Spotlight* (Feb 1951): 6–7, 57.

9. "Die Storie van die Rooibaadjie." *On Parade* 4.8 (30 May 1952): 15–16; in English as "The Red Coat", undated ms., Harry Ransom Humanities Research Center, Austin, Texas.

10. "The Question." *Personality* (14 Aug 1969): 139–141.

11. "A Boer Rip van Winkel." Undated ms., Harry Ransom Humanities Research Center, Austin, Texas; *Unto Dust*: 154–160.

THE AFFAIR AT
YSTERSPRUIT

It was in the Second Boer War, at the skirmish of Ysterspruit, near Klerksdorp, in February 1902, that Johannes Engelbrecht, eldest son of Ouma Engelbrecht, widow, received a considerable number of bullet wounds, from which he subsequently died. And when she spoke about the death of her son in battle, Ouma Engelbrecht dwelt heavily on the fact that Johannes had fought bravely. She would enumerate his wounds, and, if you were interested, she would trace in detail the direction that each bullet took through the body of her son.

If you liked stories of the past, and led her on, Ouma Engelbrecht would also mention, after a while, that she had a photograph of Johannes in her bedroom. It was with great difficulty that a stranger could get her to bring out that photograph. But she usually showed it, in the end. And then she would talk very fast about people not being able to understand the feelings that went on in a mother's heart.

"People put the photograph away from them," she would say, "and they turn it face downwards on the rusbank. And all the time I say to them, no, Johannes died bravely. I say to them that they don't know how a mother feels. One bullet came in from in front, just to the right of his heart, and it went through his gall bladder and then struck a bone in his spine and passed out through his hip. And another bullet. . . "

So she would go on while the stranger studied the photograph of her son Johannes, who died of wounds received in the skirmish at Ysterspruit.

When the talk came round to the old days, leading up to and including the Second Boer War, I was always interested when they had a photograph that I could examine, at some farmhouse in that part of the Groot Marico District that faces towards the Kalahari. And when they showed me, hanging framed against a wall of the voorkamer – or having brought it from an adjoining room – a photograph of a burgher of the South African Republic, father or son or husband or lover, then it was always with a thrill of pride in my land and my people that I looked on a likeness of a hero of the Boer War.

I would be equally interested whether it were the portrait of a bearded kommandant or of a youngster of fifteen. Or of a newly appointed veldkornet, looking important, seated on a riempiestoel with his Mauser held upright so that it would come into the photograph, but also turned slightly to the side, for fear that the muzzle should cover up part of the veldkornet's face, or a piece of his manly chest. And I would think that that veldkornet never sat so stiffly on his horse – certainly not on the morning when the commando set out for the Natal border. And he would have looked less important, although perhaps more solemn, on a night when the empty bully-beef tins rattled against the barbed wire in front of a blockhouse, and the English Lee-Metfords spat flame.

I was a school-teacher, many years ago, at a little school in the Marico Bushveld, near the border of the Bechuanaland Protectorate. The Transvaal Education Department expected me to visit the parents of the schoolchildren in the area at intervals. But even if this huisbesoek were not part of my after-school duties, I would have gone and visited the parents in any case. And when I discovered, after one or two casual calls, that the older parents were a fund of first-class story material, that they could hold the listener enthralled with tales of the past, with embroidered reminiscences of Transvaal life in the old days, then I became very conscientious about huisbesoek.

"What happened after that, Oom?" I would say, calling on a parent for about the third week in succession, "when you were trekking through the kloof that night, I mean, and you had muzzled both the black calf with the dappled belly and your daughter, so that Mojaja's men would not be able to hear anything?"

And then the oom would knock out the ash from his pipe on to his veldskoen and he would proceed to relate – his words a slow and steady rumble and with the red dust of the road in their sound, almost – a tale of terror or of high romance or of soft laughter.

It was quite by accident that I came across Ouma Engelbrecht in a two-roomed, mud-walled dwelling some little distance off the Government Road and a few hundred yards away from the homestead of her son-in-law, Stoffel Brink, on whom I had called earlier in the afternoon. I had not been in the Marico very long, then, and my interview with Stoffel Brink had been, on the whole, unsatisfactory. I wanted to know how deep the Boer trenches were dug into the foot of the koppies at Magersfontein, where Stoffel Brink had fought. Stoffel Brink, on the other hand, was anxious to learn whether, in regard to what I taught the children, I would follow the guidance of the local school committee, of which he was chairman, or whether I was one of that new kind of school-teacher who went by a little printed book of subjects supplied by the Education Department. He added that this latter class of schoolmaster was causing a lot of unpleasantness in the Bushveld through teaching the children that the earth moved round the sun, and through broaching similar questions of a political nature.

I replied evasively, with the result that Stoffel Brink launched forth for almost an hour on the merits of the old-fashioned Hollander schoolmaster, who could teach the children all he knew himself in eighteen months, because he taught them only facts.

"If a child stays at school longer than that," Stoffel Brink added, "then the rest of the time he can only learn lies."

I left about then, and on my way back, a little distance from the road and half concealed by tall bush, I found the two-roomed dwelling of Ouma Engelbrecht.

It was good, there.

I could see that Ouma Engelbrecht did not have much time for her son-in-law, Stoffel Brink. For when I mentioned his references to education, when I had merely sought to learn some details about the Boer trenches at Magersfontein, she said that maybe he could learn all there was to know in eighteen months, but he had not learnt how to be ordinarily courteous to a stranger who came to his door – a stranger, moreover, who was a schoolmaster asking information about the Boer War.

Then, of course, she spoke about her son, Johannes, who didn't have to hide in a Magersfontein trench, but who was sitting straight up on his horse when all those bullets went through him at Ysterspruit, and who died of his wounds some time later. Johannes had always been such a well-behaved boy, Ouma Engelbrecht told me, and he was gentle and kind-hearted.

She told me many stories of his childhood and early youth. She spoke about a time when the span of red Afrikaner oxen got stuck with the wagon in the drift, and her husband and the labourers, with long whip and short sjambok, could not move them – and then Johannes had come along and he had spoken softly to the red Afrikaner oxen, and he had called on each of them by name, and the team had made one last mighty effort, and had pulled the wagon through to the other side.

"And yet they never understood him in these parts," Ouma Engelbrecht continued. "They say things about him, and I hardly ever talk of him any more. And when I show them his portrait, they hardly even look at it, and they put the picture away from them, and when they are sitting on that rusbank where you are sitting now, they place the portrait of Johannes face downwards beside them."

I told Ouma Engelbrecht, laughing reassuringly the while, that I stood above the pettiness of local intrigue. I told her that I had already noticed that there were all kinds of queer undercurrents below the placid surface of life in the Groot Marico. There was the example of what had happened that very afternoon, when her son-in-law, Stoffel Brink, had conceived a nameless prejudice against me, simply because I was not prepared to teach the schoolchildren that the earth was flat. I told her that it was ridiculous to imagine that a man in my position, a man of education and wide tolerance, should allow himself to be influenced by local Dwars-berge gossip.

Ouma Engelbrecht spoke freely, then, and the fight at Ysterspruit lived for me again – Kemp and De la Rey and the captured English convoy, the ambush and the booty of a million rounds of ammunition. It was almost as though the affair at Ysterspruit was being related to me, not by a lone-ly woman whose son received his death wounds on the vlaktes near Klerks-dorp, but by a burgher who had taken a prominent part in the battle.

And so, naturally, I wanted to see the photograph of her son, Johannes Engelbrecht.

When it came to the Boer War (although I did not say that to Ouma Engelbrecht), I didn't care if a Boer commander was not very competent or very cunning in his strategy, or if a burgher was not particularly brave. It was enough for me that he had fought. And to me General Snyman, for instance, in spite of the history books' somewhat unflattering assessment of his military qualities, was a hero, nonetheless. I had seen General Snyman's photograph, somewhere: that face that was like Transvaal blouklip; those eyes that had no fire in them, but a stubborn and elemental strength. You still see Boers in the backveld with that look today.

In my mind I had contrasted the portraits of General Snyman and Comte de Villebois Mareuil, the Frenchman who had come all the way from Europe to shoulder a Mauser for the Transvaal Republic. De Villebois, poet and romantic, last-ditch champion of the forlorn hope and the heroic cause. . . Oh, they were very different, these two men, De Villebois Mareuil, the French nobleman, and Snyman, the Boer. But I had an equal admiration for them both.

Anyway, it was well on towards evening when Ouma Engelbrecht, yielding at last to my cajoleries and entreaties, got up slowly from her chair and went into the adjoining room. She returned with a photograph enclosed in a heavy black frame. I waited, tense with curiosity, to see the portrait of that son of hers who had died of wounds at Ysterspruit, and whose reputation the loose prattle of the neighbourhood had invested with a dishonour as dark as the frame about his photograph.

Flicking a few specks of dust from the portrait, Ouma Engelbrecht handed over the picture to me.

And she was still talking about the things that went on in a mother's heart, things of pride and sorrow that the world did not understand, when, in an unconscious reaction, hardly aware of what I was doing, I placed beside me on the rusbank, face downwards, the photograph of a young man whose hat brim was cocked on the right side, jauntily, and whose jacket with narrow lapels was buttoned up high. With a queer jumble of inarticulate feelings I realised that, in the affair at Ysterspruit, they were all Mauser bullets that had passed through the youthful body of Johannes Engelbrecht, National Scout.

Yellow Moepels

If ever you spoke to my father about witch-doctors (Oom Schalk Lourens said), he would always relate one story. And at the end of it he would explain that, while a witch-doctor could foretell the future for you from the bones, at the same time he could only tell you the things that didn't matter. My father used to say that the important things were as much hidden from the witch-doctor as from the man who listened to his prophecy.

My father said that when he was sixteen he went with his friend, Paul, a stripling of about his own age, to a kaffir witch-doctor. They had heard that this witch-doctor was very good at throwing the bones.

This witch-doctor lived alone in a mud hut. While they were still on the way to the hut the two youths laughed and jested, but as soon as they got inside they felt different. They were impressed. The witch-doctor was very old and very wrinkled. He had on a queer head-dress made up from the tails of different wild animals.

You could tell that the boys were overawed as they sat there on the floor in the dark. Because my father, who had meant to hand the witch-doctor only a plug of Boer tobacco, gave him a whole roll. And Paul, who had said, when they were outside, that he was going to give him nothing at all, actually handed over his hunting knife.

Then he threw the bones. He threw first for my father. He told him many things. He told him that he would grow up to be a good burgher, and that he would one day be very prosperous. He would have a big farm and many cattle and two ox-wagons.

But what the witch-doctor did not tell my father was that in years to come he would have a son, Schalk, who could tell better stories than any man in the Marico.

Then the witch-doctor threw the bones for Paul. For a long while he was silent. He looked from the bones to Paul, and back to the bones, in a strange way. Then he spoke.

"I can see you go far away, my kleinbaas," he said, "very far away over the great waters. Away from your own land, my kleinbaas."

"And the veld," Paul asked, "and the krantzes and the vlaktes?"

"And away from your own people," the witch-doctor said.

"And will I – will I – "

"No, my kleinbasie," the witch-doctor answered, "you will not come back. You will die there."

My father said that when they came out of that hut Paul Kruger's face was very white. That was why my father used to say that, while a witch-doctor could tell you true things, he could not tell you the things that really mattered.

And my father was right.

Take the case of Neels Potgieter and Martha Rossouw, for instance. They became engaged to be married just before the affair at Paardekraal. There, on the hoogte, our leaders pointed out to us that, although the Transvaal had been annexed by Sir Theophilus Shepstone, it nevertheless meant that we would have to go on paying taxes just the same. Everybody knew then that it was war.

Neels Potgieter and I were in the same commando.

It was arranged that the burghers of the neighbourhood should assemble at the veldkornet's house. Instructions had also been given that no women were to be present. There was much fighting to be done, and this final leave-taking was likely to be an embarrassing thing.

Nevertheless, as always, the women came. And among them was Neels's sweetheart, Martha Rossouw. And also there was my sister, Annie.

I shall never forget that scene in front of the veldkornet's house, in the early morning, when there were still shadows on the rante, and a thin wind blew through the grass. We had no predikant there; but an ouderling, with two bandoliers slung across his body, and a Martini in his hand, said a few words. He was a strong and simple man, with no great gifts of oratory. But when he spoke about the Transvaal we could feel what was in his heart, and we took off our hats in silence.

And it was not long afterwards that I again took off my hat in much the same way. Then it was at Majuba Hill. It was after the battle, and the ouderling still had his two bandoliers around him when we buried him at the foot of the koppie.

But what impressed me most was the prayer that followed the ouderling's brief address. In front of the veldkornet's house we knelt, each burgher with his rifle at his side. And the womenfolk knelt down with us. And the wind seemed very gentle as it stirred the tall grass-blades; very gentle as it swept over the bared heads of the men and fluttered the kappies and skirts of the women; very gentle as it carried the prayers of our nation over the veld.

After that we stood up and sang a hymn. The ceremony was over. The agterryers brought us our horses. And, dry-eyed and tight-lipped, each woman sent her man forth to war. There was no weeping.

Then, in accordance with Boer custom, we fired a volley into the air. "Voorwaarts, burghers," came the veldkornet's order, and we cantered down the road in twos. But before we left I had overheard Neels Potgieter say something to Martha Rossouw as he leant out of the saddle and kissed her. My sister Annie, standing beside my horse, also heard.

"When the moepels are ripe, Martha," Neels said, "I will come to you again."

Annie and I looked at each other and smiled. It was a pretty thing that Neels had said. But then Martha was also pretty. More pretty than the veld-trees that bore those yellow moepels, I reflected – and more wild.

I was still thinking of this when our commando had passed over the bult, in a long line, on our way to the south, where Natal was, and the other commandos, and Majuba.

This was the war of Bronkhorstspruit and General Colley and Laing's Nek. You have no doubt heard many accounts of this war, some of them truthful, perhaps. For it is a singular thing that, as a man grows older, and looks back on fights that he has been in, he keeps on remembering, each year, more and more of the enemy that he has shot.

Klaas Uys was a man like that. Each year, on his birthday, he remembered one or two more redcoats that he had shot, whereupon he got up straight away and put another few notches in the wood part of his rifle, along the barrel. And he said his memory was getting better every year.

All the time I was on commando, I received only one letter. That came from Annie, my sister. She said I was not to take any risks, and that I must keep far away from the English, especially if they had guns. She also said I was to remember that I was a white man, and that if there was any dangerous work to be done, I had to send a kaffir out to do it.

There were more things like that in Annie's letter. But I had no need of her advice. Our kommandant was a God-fearing and wily man, and he knew even better ways than Annie did for keeping out of range of the enemy's fire.

But Annie also said, at the end of her letter, that she and Martha Rossouw had gone to a witch-doctor. They had gone to find out about Neels Potgieter and me. Now, if I had been at home, I would not have permitted Annie to indulge in this nonsense.

Especially as the witch-doctor said to her, "Yes, missus, I can see Baas Schalk Lourens. He will come back safe. He is very clever, Baas Schalk. He lies behind a big stone, with a dirty brown blanket pulled over his head. And he stays behind that stone until the fighting is finished – quite finished."

According to Annie's letter, the witch-doctor told her a few other things about me, too. But I won't bother to repeat them now. I think I have said enough to show you what sort of a scoundrel that old kaffir was. He not only took advantage of the credulity of a simple girl, but he also tried to be funny at the expense of a young man who was fighting for his country's freedom.

What was more, Annie said that she had recognised it was me right away, just from the kaffir's description of that blanket.

To Martha Rossouw the witch-doctor said, "Baas Neels Potgieter will come back to you, missus, when the moepels are ripe again. At sun-under he will come."

That was all he said about Neels, and there wasn't very much in that, anyway, seeing that Neels himself – except for the bit about the sunset – had made the very same prophecy the day the commando set out. I suppose that witch-doctor had been too busy thinking out foolish and spiteful things about me to be able to give any attention to Neels Potgieter's affairs.

But I didn't mention Annie's letter to Neels. He might have wanted to know more than I was willing to tell him. More, even, perhaps, than Martha was willing to tell him – Martha of the wild heart.

Then, at last, the war ended, and over the Transvaal the Vierkleur waved again. And the commandos went home by their different ways. And our leaders revived their old quarrels as to who should be president. And, everywhere, except for a number of lonely graves on hillside and vlakte, things were as they had been before Shepstone came.

It was getting on towards evening when our small band rode over the bult again, and once more came to a halt at the veldkornet's house. A messenger had been sent on in advance to announce our coming, and from far around the women and children and old men had gathered to welcome their victorious burghers back from the war. And there were tears in many eyes when we sang, "Hef, Burghers, hef."

And the moepels were ripe and yellow on the trees.

And in the dusk Neels Potgieter found Martha Rossouw and kissed her. At sundown, as the witch-doctor had said. But there was one important thing that the witch-doctor had not told. It was something that Neels Potgieter did not know, either, just then. And that was that Martha did not want him any more.

THE RED COAT

I have spoken before of the some of the queer things that happen to your mind through fever (Oom Schalk Lourens said). In the past there was a good deal more fever in the Marico and Waterberg Districts than there is today. And you got it in a more severe form, too. Today you still get malaria in these parts, of course. But your temperature doesn't go so high any more before the fever breaks. And you are not left as weak after an attack of malaria as you were in the old days. Nor do you often get illusions of the sort that afterwards came to trouble the mind of Andries Visagie.

They say that this improvement is due to civilisation.

Well, I suppose that must be right. For one thing, we now have a Government lorry from Zeerust every week with letters and newspapers and catalogues from Johannesburg shopkeepers. And only three years ago Jurie Bekker bought a wooden stand with a glass for measuring how much rain he gets on his farm. Jurie Bekker is very proud of his rain-gauge, too, and will accompany any white visitor to the back of his house to show him how well it works. "We have had no rain for the last three years," Jurie Bekker will explain, "and that is exactly what the rain-gauge records, also. Look, you can see for yourself – nil!"

Jurie Bekker also tried to explain the rain instrument to the kaffirs on his farm. But he gave it up. "A kaffir with a blanket on hasn't got the brain to understand a white man's inventions," Jurie Bekker said about it, afterwards. "When I showed my kaffirs what this rain-gauge was all about, they just stood in a long row and laughed."

Nevertheless, I must admit that, with all this civilisation we are getting here, the malaria fever has not of recent years been the scourge it was in the old days.

The story of Andries Visagie and his fever begins at the battle of Bronkhorstspruit. It was at the battle of Bronkhorstspruit that Andries Visagie had his life saved by Piet Niemand, according to all accounts.

And yet it was also arising out of that incident that many people in this part of the Marico in later years came to the conclusion that Andries Visagie was somebody whose word you could not take seriously, because of the suffering that he had undergone.

You know, of course, that the Bronkhorstspruit battle was fought very long ago. In those days we still called the English 'redcoats'. For the English soldiers wore red jackets that we could see against the khaki colour of the tamboekie grass for almost as far as the bullets from our Martini-Henry rifles could carry. That shows you how uncivilised those times were.

I often heard Piet Niemand relate the story of how he found Andries Visagie lying unconscious in a donga on the battlefield, and of how he revived him with brandy that he had in his water-bottle.

Piet Niemand explained that, from the number of redcoats that were lined up at Bronkhorstspruit that morning, he could see it was going to be a serious engagement, and so he had thoughtfully emptied all the water out of his bottle and had replaced it with Magaliesberg peach brandy of the rawest kind he could get. Piet Niemand said that he was advancing against the English when he came across that donga. He was advancing very fast and was looking neither to right nor left of him, he said. And he would draw lines on any piece of paper that was handy to show you the direction he took.

I can still remember how annoyed we all were when a young school-teacher, looking intently at that piece of paper, said that if that was the direction in which Piet Niemand was advancing, then it must have meant that the English had got right to behind the Boer lines, which was contrary to what he had read in the history books. Shortly afterwards Hannes Potgieter, who was chairman of our school committee, got that young school-teacher transferred.

As Hannes Potgieter said, that young school-teacher with his history-book ideas had never been in a battle and didn't know what real fighting was. In the confusion of a fight, with guns going off all round you, Hannes Potgieter declared, it was not unusual for a burgher to find himself advancing away from the enemy – and quite fast, too.

He was not ashamed to admit that a very similar thing had happened to him at one stage of the battle of Majuba Hill. He had run back a long way, because he had suddenly felt that he wanted to make sure that the kaffir agterryers were taking proper care of the horses. But he need have had no fears on that score, Hannes Potgieter added. Because when he reached the sheltered spot among the thorn-trees where the horses were tethered, he found that three kommandants and a veldkornet had arrived there before him, on the same errand. The veldkornet was so anxious to reassure himself that the horses were all right, that he was even trying to mount one of them.

When Hannes Potgieter said that, he winked. And we all laughed. For we knew that he had fought bravely at Majuba Hill. But he was also ready always to acknowledge that he had been very frightened at Majuba Hill. And because he had been in several wars, he did not like to hear the courage of Piet Niemand called in question. What Hannes Potgieter meant us to understand was that if, at the battle of Bronkhorstspruit, Piet Niemand did perhaps run at one stage, it was the sort of thing that could happen to any man; and for which any man could be forgiven, too.

And, in any case, Piet Niemand's story was interesting enough. He said that in the course of his advance he came across a donga, on the edge of which a thorn-bush was growing. The donga was about ten foot deep. He descended into the donga to light his pipe. He couldn't light his pipe out there on the open veld, because it was too windy, he said. When he reached the bottom of the donga, he also found that he had brought most of that thorn-bush along with him.

Then, in a bend of the donga, Piet Niemand saw what he thought was an English soldier, lying face downwards. He thought, at first, that the English soldier had come down there to light his pipe, also, and had decided to stay longer. He couldn't see too clearly, Piet Niemand said, because the smoke of the battle of Bronkhorstspruit had got into his eyes. Maybe the smoke from his pipe, too, I thought. That is, if what he was lighting up there in the donga was Piet Retief roll tobacco.

Why Piet Niemand thought that the man lying at the bend of the donga was an Englishman was because he was wearing a red coat. But in the next moment Piet Niemand realised that the man was not an Englishman. For the man's neck was not also red.

Immediately there flashed into Piet Niemand's mind the suspicion that the man was a Boer in English uniform – a Transvaal Boer fighting against his own people. If it had been an Englishman lying there, he would have called on him to surrender, Piet Niemand said, but a Boer traitor he was going to shoot without giving him a chance to get up.

He was in the act of raising his Martini-Henry to fire, when the truth came to him. And that was how he first met Andries Visagie and how he came to save his life. He saw that while Andries Visagie's coat was indeed red, it was not with dye, but with the blood from his wound. Piet Niemand said that he was so overcome at the thought of the sin he had been about to commit that when he unstrapped his water-bottle his knees trembled as much as did his fingers. But when Piet Niemand told this part of his story, Hannes Potgieter said that he need not make any excuses for himself, especially as no harm had come of it. If it had been a Boer traitor instead of Piet Niemand who had found himself in that same situation, Hannes Potgieter said, then the Boer traitor would have fired in any case, without bothering very much as to whether it was a Boer or an Englishman that he was shooting.

Piet Niemand knelt down beside Andries Visagie and turned him round and succeeded in pouring a quantity of brandy down his throat. Andries Visagie was not seriously wounded, but he had a high fever, from the sun and through loss of blood, and he spoke strange words.

That was the story that Piet Niemand had to tell.

Afterwards Andries Visagie made a good recovery in the mill at Bronkhorstspruit, that the kommandant had turned into a hospital. And they say it was very touching to observe Andries Visagie's gratitude when Piet Niemand came to visit him.

Andries Visagie lay on the floor, on a rough mattress filled with grass and dried mealie-leaves. Piet Niemand went and sat on the floor beside him. They conversed. By that time Andries Visagie had recovered sufficiently to remember that he had shot three redcoats for sure. He added, however, that as a result of the weakness caused by his wound, his mind was not very clear, at times. But when he got quite well and strong again, he would remember better. And then he would not be at all surprised if he remembered that he had also shot a general, he said.

Piet Niemand then related some of his own acts of bravery. And because they were both young men it gave them much pleasure to pass themselves off as heroes in each other's company.

Piet Niemand had already stood up to go when Andries Visagie reached his hand underneath the mattress and pulled out a watch with a heavy gold chain. The watch was shaped like an egg and on the case were pictures of angels, painted in enamel. Even without those angels, it would have been a very magnificent watch. But with those angels painted on the case, you would not care much if the watch did not go, even, and you still had to tell the time from the sun, holding your hand cupped over your eyes.

"I inherited this watch from my grandfather," Andries Visagie said. "He brought it with him on the Great Trek. You saved my life in the donga. You must take this watch as a keepsake."

Those who were present at this incident in the temporary hospital at Bronkhorstspruit said that Piet Niemand reached over to receive the gift. He almost had his hand on the watch, they say. And then he changed his mind and stood up straight.

"What I did was nothing," Piet Niemand said. "It was something anybody would have done. Anybody that was brave enough, I mean. But I want no reward for it. Maybe I'll some day buy myself a watch like that."

Andries Visagie kept his father's father's egg-shaped watch, after all. But in his having offered Piet Niemand his most treasured possession, and in Piet Niemand having declined to accept it, there was set the seal on the friendship of those two young men. This friendship was guarded, maybe, by the wings of the angels painted in enamel on the watch-case. Afterwards people were to say that it was a pity Andries Visagie should have turned so queer in the head. It must have been that he had suffered too much, these people said.

In gratitude for their services in the First Boer War, the Government of the Transvaal Republic made grants of farming land in the Waterberg district to those Boers on commando who had no ground of their own. The Government of the Transvaal Republic did not think it necessary to explain that the area in question was already occupied – by lions and malaria mosquitoes and hostile kaffirs. Nevertheless, many Boers knew the facts about that part of the Waterberg pretty well. So only a handful of burghers were prepared to accept Government farms. Most of the others felt that, seeing they had just come out of one war, there was not much point in going straight back into another.

All the same, a number of burghers did go and take up land in that area, and to everybody's surprise – not least to the surprise of the Government, I suppose – they fared reasonably well. And among those new settlers in the Waterberg were Piet Niemand and Andries Visagie. Their farms were not more than two days' journey apart. So you could almost say they were neighbours. They visited each other regularly.

The years went by, and then in a certain wet season Andries Visagie lay stricken with malaria. And in his delirium he said strange things. Fancying himself back again at Bronkhorstspruit, Andries Visagie said he could remember the long line of English generals he was shooting. He was shooting them full of medals, he said.

But there was another thing that Andries Visagie said he remembered then. And after he recovered from the malaria he still insisted that the circumstance he had recalled during his illness was the truth. He said that through that second bout of fever he was able to remember what had happened years before, in the donga, when he was also delirious.

And it was then that many of the farmers in the Waterberg began to say what a pity it was that Andries Visagie's illness should so far have affected his mind.

For Andries Visagie said that he could remember distinctly, now, that time when he was lying in the donga. And he would never, of course, know who shot him. But what he did remember was that when Piet Niemand was bending over him, holding a water-bottle in his hand, Piet Niemand was wearing a red coat.

FUNERAL EARTH

We had a difficult task, that time (Oom Schalk Lourens said), teaching Sijefu's tribe of Mtosas to become civilised. But they did not show any appreciation. Even after we had set fire to their huts in a long row round the slopes of Abjaterskop, so that you could see the smoke almost as far as Nietverdiend, the Mtosas remained just about as unenlightened as ever. They would retreat into the mountains, where it was almost impossible for our commando to follow them on horseback. They remained hidden in the thick bush.

"I can sense these kaffirs all around us," Veldkornet Andries Joubert said to our seksie of about a dozen burghers when we had come to a halt in a clearing amid the tall withaaks. "I have been in so many kaffir wars that I can almost *smell* when there are kaffirs lying in wait for us with assegais. And yet all day long you never see a single Mtosa that you can put a lead bullet through."

He also said that if this war went on much longer we would forget altogether how to handle a gun. And what would we do then, when we again had to fight England?

Young Fanie Louw, who liked saying funny things, threw back his head and pretended to be sniffing the air with discrimination. "I can smell a whole row of assegais with broad blades and short handles," Fanie Louw said. "The stabbing assegai has got more of a selon's rose sort of smell about it than a throwing spear. The selon's rose that you come across in graveyards."

The veldkornet did not think Fanie Louw's remark very funny, however. And he said we all knew that this was the first time Fanie Louw had ever been on commando. He also said that if a crowd of Mtosas were to leap out of the bush on to us suddenly, then you wouldn't be able to smell Fanie Louw for dust. The veldkornet also said another thing that was even better.

Our group of burghers laughed heartily. Maybe Veldkornet Joubert could not think out a lot of nonsense to say just on the spur of the moment, in the way that Fanie Louw could, but give our veldkornet a chance to reflect, first, and he would come out with the kind of remark that you just had to admire.

Indeed, from the very next thing Veldkornet Joubert said, you could see how deep was his insight. And he did not have to think much, either, then.

"Let us get out of here as quick as hell, men," he said, speaking very distinctly. "Perhaps the kaffirs are hiding out in the open turf lands, where there are no trees. And none of this long tamboekie grass, either."

When we emerged from that stretch of bush we were glad to discover that our veldkornet had been right, like always.

For another group of Transvaal burghers had hit on the same strategy.

"We were in the middle of the bush," their leader, Combrinck, said to us, after we had exchanged greetings. "A very thick part of the bush, with withaaks standing up like skeletons. And we suddenly thought the Mtosas might have gone into hiding out here in the open."

You could see that Veldkornet Joubert was pleased to think that he had, on his own, worked out the same tactics as Combrinck, who was known as a skilful kaffir-fighter. All the same, it seemed as though this was going to be a long war.

It was then that, again speaking out of his turn, Fanie Louw said that all we needed now was for the kommandant himself to arrive there in the middle of the turf lands with the main body of burghers. "Maybe we should even go back to Pretoria to see if the Mtosas aren't perhaps hiding in the Volksraad," he said. "Passing laws and things. You know how cheeky a Mtosa is."

"It can't be worse than some of the laws that the Volksraad is already passing now," Combrinck said, gruffly. From that we could see that why he had not himself been appointed kommandant was because he had voted against the President in the last elections.

By that time the sun was sitting not more than about two Cape feet above a tall koppie on the horizon. Accordingly, we started looking about for a place to camp. It was muddy in the turf lands, and there was no fire-wood there, but we all said that we did not mind. We would not pamper ourselves by going to sleep in the thick bush, we told one another. It was war-time, and we were on commando, and the mud of the turf lands was good enough for *us*, we said.

It was then that an unusual thing happened.

For we suddenly did see Mtosas. We saw them from a long way off. They came out of the bush and marched right out into the open. They made no attempt to hide. We saw in amazement that they were coming straight in our direction, advancing in single file. And we observed, even from that distance, that they were unarmed. Instead of assegais and shields they carried burdens on their heads. And almost at the same moment we realised, from the heavy look of those burdens, that the carriers must be women.

For that reason we took our guns in our hands and stood waiting. Since it was women, we were naturally prepared for the lowest form of treachery.

As the column drew nearer we saw that at the head of it was Ndambe, an old native whom we knew well. For years he had been Sijefu's chief counsellor. Ndambe held up his hand. The line of women halted. Ndambe spoke. He declared that we white men were kings among kings and elephants among elephants. He also said that we were ringhals snakes more poisonous and generally disgusting than any ringhals snake in the country.

We knew, of course, that Ndambe was only paying us compliments in his ignorant Mtosa fashion. And so we naturally felt highly gratified. I can still remember the way Jurie Bekker nudged me in the ribs and said, "Did you hear that?"

When Ndambe went on, however, to say that we were filthier than the spittle of the green tree-toad, several burghers grew restive. They felt that there was perhaps such a thing as carrying these tribal courtesies a bit too far.

It was then that Veldkornet Joubert, slipping his finger inside the trigger guard of his gun, requested Ndambe to come to the point. By the expression on our veldkornet's face, you could see that he had had enough of compliments for one day.

They had come to offer peace, Ndambe told us then.

What the women carried on their heads were presents.

At a sign from Ndambe the column knelt in the mud of the turf land. They brought lion and zebra skins and elephant tusks, and beads and brass bangles and, on a long grass mat, the whole haunch of a red Afrikaner ox, hide and hoof and all. And several pigs cut in half. And clay pots filled to the brim with white beer, and also – and this we prized most – witch-doctor medicines that protected you against goël spirits at night and the evil eye.

Ndambe gave another signal. A woman with a clay pot on her head rose up from the kneeling column and advanced towards us. We saw then that what she had in the pot was black earth. It was wet and almost like turf soil. We couldn't understand what they wanted to bring us that for. As though we didn't have enough of it, right there where we were standing, and sticking to our veldskoens, and all. And yet Ndambe acted as though that was the most precious part of the peace offerings that his chief, Sijefu, had sent us.

It was when Ndambe spoke again that we saw how ignorant he and his chief and the whole Mtosa tribe were, really.

He took a handful of soil out of the pot and pressed it together between his fingers. Then he told us how honoured the Mtosa tribe was because we were waging war against them. In the past they had only had flat-faced Mshangaans with spiked knobkerries to fight against, he said, but now it was different. Our veldkornet took half a step forward, then, in case Ndambe was going to start flattering us again. So Ndambe said, simply, that the Mtosas would be glad if we came and made war against them later on, when the harvests had been gathered in. But in the meantime the tribe did not wish to continue fighting.

It was the time for sowing.

Ndambe let the soil run through his fingers, to show us how good it was. He also invited us to taste it. We declined.

We accepted the presents and peace was made. And I can still remember how Veldkornet Joubert shook his head and said, "Can you beat the Mtosas for ignorance?"

And I can still remember what Jurie Bekker said, also. That was when something made him examine the haunch of beef more closely, and he found his own brand mark on it.

It was not long afterwards that the war came against England.

By the end of the second year of the war the Boer forces were in a very bad way. But we would not make peace. Veldkornet Joubert was now promoted to kommandant. Combrinck fell in the battle before Dalmanutha. Jurie Bekker was still with us. And so was Fanie Louw. And it was strange how attached we had grown to Fanie Louw during the years of hardship that we went through together in the field. But up to the end we had to admit that, while we had got used to his jokes, and we knew there was no harm in them, we would have preferred it that he should stop making them.

He did stop, and for ever, in a skirmish near a blockhouse. We buried him in the shade of a thorn-tree. We got ready to fill in his grave, after which the kommandant would say a few words and we would bare our heads and sing a psalm. As you know, it was customary at a funeral for each mourner to take up a handful of earth and fling it in the grave.

When Kommandant Joubert stooped down and picked up his handful of earth, a strange thing happened. And I remembered that other war, against the Mtosas. And we knew – although we would not say it – what was now that longing in the hearts of each of us. For Kommandant Joubert did not straightway drop the soil into Fanie Louw's grave. Instead, he kneaded the damp ground between his fingers. It was as though he had forgotten that it was funeral earth. He seemed to be thinking not of death, then, but of life.

We patterned after him, picking up handfuls of soil and pressing it together. We felt the deep loam in it, and saw how springy it was, and we let it trickle through our fingers. And we could remember only that it was the time for sowing.

I understood then how, in an earlier war, the Mtosas had felt, they who were also farmers.

MAFEKING ROAD

When people ask me – as they often do – how it is that I can tell the best stories of anybody in the Transvaal (Oom Schalk Lourens said, modestly), then I explain to them that I just learn through observing the way that the world has with men and women. When I say this they nod their heads wisely, and say that they understand, and I nod my head wisely also, and that seems to satisfy them. But the thing I say to them is a lie, of course.

For it is not the story that counts. What matters is the way you tell it. The important thing is to know just at what moment you must knock out your pipe on your veldskoen, and at what stage of the story you must start talking about the School Committee at Drogevlei. Another necessary thing is to know what part of the story to leave out.

And you can never learn these things.

Look at Floris, the last of the Van Barnevelts. There is no doubt that he had a good story, and he should have been able to get people to listen to it. And yet nobody took any notice of him or of the things he had to say. Just because he couldn't tell the story properly.

Accordingly, it made me sad whenever I listened to him talk. For I could tell just where he went wrong. He never knew the moment at which to knock the ash out of his pipe. He always mentioned his opinion of the Drogevlei School Committee in the wrong place. And, what was still worse, he didn't know what part of the story to leave out.

And it was no use my trying to teach him, because as I have said, this is the thing that you can never learn. And so, each time he had told his story, I would see him turn away from me, with a look of doom on his face, and walk slowly down the road, stoop-shouldered, the last of the Van Barnevelts.

On the wall of Floris's voorkamer is a long family tree of the Van Barnevelts. You can see it there for yourself. It goes back for over two hundred years, to the Van Barnevelts of Amsterdam. At one time it went even further back, but that was before the white ants started on the top part of it and ate away quite a lot of Van Barnevelts. Nevertheless, if you look at this list, you will notice that at the bottom, under Floris's own name, there is the last entry, "Stephanus." And behind the name, "Stephanus," between two bent strokes, you will read the words: "Obiit Mafeking."

At the outbreak of the Second Boer War Floris van Barnevelt was a widower, with one son, Stephanus, who was aged seventeen. The commando from our part of the Transvaal set off very cheerfully. We made a fine show, with our horses and our wide hats and our bandoliers, and with the sun shining on the barrels of our Mausers.

Young Stephanus van Barnevelt was the gayest of us all. But he said there was one thing he didn't like about the war, and that was that, in the end, we would have to go over the sea. He said that, after we had invaded the whole of the Cape, our commando would have to go on a ship and invade England also.

But we didn't go overseas, just then. Instead, our veldkornet told us that the burghers from our part had been ordered to join the big commando that was lying at Mafeking. We had to go and shoot a man there called Baden-Powell.

We rode steadily on into the west. After a while we noticed that our veldkornet frequently got off his horse and engaged in conversation with passing kaffirs, leading them some distance from the roadside and speaking earnestly to them. Of course, it was right that our veldkornet should explain to the kaffirs that it was war-time, now, and that the Republic expected every kaffir to stop smoking so much dagga and to think seriously about what was going on. But we noticed that each time at the end of the conversation the kaffir would point towards something, and that our veldkornet would take much pains to follow the direction of the kaffir's finger.

Of course, we understood, then, what it was all about. Our veldkornet was a young fellow, and he was shy to let us see that he didn't know the way to Mafeking.

Somehow, after that, we did not have so much confidence in our veldkornet.

After a few days we got to Mafeking. We stayed there a long while, until the English troops came up and relieved the place. We left, then. We left quickly. The English troops had brought a lot of artillery with them. And if we had difficulty in finding the road to Mafeking, we had no difficulty in finding the road away from Mafeking. And this time our veldkornet did not need kaffirs, either, to point with their fingers where we had to go. Even though we did a lot of travelling in the night.

Long afterwards I spoke to an Englishman about this. He said it gave him a queer feeling to hear about the other side of the story of Mafeking. He said there had been very great rejoicings in England when Mafeking was relieved, and it was strange to think of the other aspect of it – of a defeated country and of broken columns blundering through the dark.

I remember many things that happened on the way back from Mafeking. There was no moon. And the stars shone down fitfully on the road that was full of guns and frightened horses and desperate men. The veld throbbed with the hoof-beats of baffled commandos. The stars looked down on scenes that told sombrely of a nation's ruin; they looked on the muzzles of the Mausers that had failed the Transvaal for the first time.

Of course, as a burgher of the Republic, I knew what my duty was. And that was to get as far away as I could from the place where, in the sunset, I had last seen English artillery. The other burghers knew their duty also. Our kommandants and veldkornets had to give very few orders. Nevertheless, although I rode very fast, there was one young man who rode still faster. He kept ahead of me all the time. He rode, as a burgher should ride when there may be stray bullets flying, with his head well down and with his arms almost round the horse's neck.

He was Stephanus, the young son of Floris van Barnevelt.

There was much grumbling and dissatisfaction, some time afterwards, when our leaders started making an effort to get the commandos in order again. In the end they managed to get us to halt. But most of us felt that this was a foolish thing to do. Especially as there was still a lot of firing going on, all over the place, in haphazard fashion, and we couldn't tell how far the English had followed us in the dark. Furthermore, the commandos had scattered in so many different directions that it seemed hopeless to try and get them together again until after the war. Stephanus and

I dismounted and stood by our horses. Soon there was a large body of men around us. Their figures looked strange and shadowy in the starlight. Some of them stood by their horses. Others sat on the grass by the roadside. "Vas staan, burghers, vas staan," came the commands of our officers. And all the time we could still hear what sounded a lot like lyddite. It seemed foolish to be waiting there.

"The next they'll want," Stephanus van Barnevelt said, "is for us to go back to Mafeking. Perhaps our kommandant has left his tobacco pouch behind, there."

Some of us laughed at this remark, but Floris, who had not dismounted, said that Stephanus ought to be ashamed of himself for talking like that. From what we could see of Floris in the gloom, he looked quite impressive, sitting very straight in the saddle, with the stars shining on his beard and rifle.

"If the veldkornet told me to go back to Mafeking," Floris said, "I would go back."

"That's how a burgher should talk," the veldkornet said, feeling flattered. For he had had little authority since the time we found out what he was talking to the kaffirs for.

"I wouldn't go back to Mafeking for anybody," Stephanus replied, "unless, maybe, it's to hand myself over to the English."

"We can shoot you for doing that," the veldkornet said. "It's contrary to military law."

"I wish I knew something about military law," Stephanus answered. "Then I would draw up a peace treaty between Stephanus van Barnevelt and England."

Some of the men laughed again. But Floris shook his head sadly. He said the Van Barnevelts had fought bravely against Spain in a war that lasted eighty years.

Suddenly, out of the darkness there came a sharp rattle of musketry, and our men started getting uneasy again. But the sound of the firing decided Stephanus. He jumped on his horse quickly.

"I am turning back," he said, "I am going to hands-up to the English."

"No, don't go," the veldkornet called to him lamely, "or at least, wait until the morning. They may shoot you in the dark by mistake." As I have said, the veldkornet had very little authority.

Two days passed before we again saw Floris van Barnevelt. He was in a very worn and troubled state, and he said that it had been very hard for him to find his way back to us.

"You should have asked the kaffirs," one of our number said with a laugh. "All the kaffirs know our veldkornet."

But Floris did not speak about what happened that night, when we saw him riding out under the starlight, following after his son and shouting to him to be a man and to fight for his country. Also, Floris did not mention Stephanus again, his son who was not worthy to be a Van Barnevelt.

After that we got separated. Our veldkornet was the first to be taken prisoner. And I often felt that he must feel very lonely on St. Helena. Because there were no kaffirs from whom he could ask the way out of the barbed-wire camp.

Then, at last our leaders came together at Vereeniging, and peace was made. And we returned to our farms, relieved that the war was over, but with heavy hearts at the thought that it had all been for nothing and that over the Transvaal the Vierkleur would not wave again.

And Floris van Barnevelt put back in its place, on the wall of the voorkamer, the copy of his family tree that had been carried with him in his knapsack throughout the war. Then a new schoolmaster came to this part of the Marico, and after a long talk with Floris, the schoolmaster wrote behind Stephanus's name, between two curved lines, the two words that you can still read there: "Obiit Mafeking."

Consequently, if you ask any person hereabouts what "obiit" means, he is able to tell you, right away, that it is a foreign word, and that it means to ride up to the English, holding your Mauser in the air, with a white flag tied to it, near the muzzle.

But it was long afterwards that Floris van Barnevelt started telling his story.

And then they took no notice of him. And they wouldn't allow him to be nominated for the Drogevlei School Committee on the grounds that a man must be wrong in the head to talk in such an irresponsible fashion.

But I knew that Floris had a good story, and that its only fault was that he told it badly. He mentioned the Drogevlei School Committee too soon. And he knocked the ash out of his pipe in the wrong place. And he always insisted on telling that part of the story that he should have left out.

THE QUESTION

Stefanus Malherbe had difficulty in getting access to the president, to put to him the question of which we were all anxious to learn the answer.

It was at Waterval Onder and President Kruger was making preparations to leave for Europe to enlist the help of foreign countries in the Transvaal's struggle against England. General Louis Botha had just been defeated at Dalmanutha. Accordingly, we who were the last of the Boer commandos in the field found ourselves hemmed in against the Portuguese border by the British forces, the few miles of railway line from Nelspruit to Komatipoort being all that still remained to us of Transvaal soil. The Boer War had hardly begun, and it already looked like the end.

But when we had occasion to watch, from a considerable distance, a column of British dragoons advancing through a half-mile stretch of bush country, there were those of us who realised that the Boer War might, after all, not be over yet. It took the column two hours to get through that bush.

Although we who served under Veldkornet Stefanus Malherbe were appointed to the duty of guarding President Kruger during those last days, we had neither the opportunity nor the temerity to talk to him in that house at Waterval Onder. For one thing, there were those men with big stomachs and heavy gold watch-chains all crowding around the president with papers they wanted him to sign. Nevertheless, when the news came that the English had broken through at Dalmanutha we overheard some of those men say, not raising their voices unduly, that something or other was no longer worth the paper it was written on. Next morning, when President Kruger again came on the front stoep of the house, alone this time, we were for the first time able to see him clearly, instead of through the thick screen of grey smoke being blown into his face from imported cigars.

"Well," Thys Haasbroek said, "I hope the president when he gets to

Europe enlists the right kind of foreigners to come and fight for the Republic. It would be too bad if he came back with another crowd of uitlanders with big stomachs and watch-chains, waving papers for concessions."

I mention this remark made by one of the burghers then at Waterval Onder with the president to show you that there was not a uniform spirit of bitter-end loyalty animating the 3 000 men who saw day by day the net of the enemy getting more tightly drawn around them. Indeed, speaking for myself, I must confess that the enthusiasm of those of our leaders who at intervals addressed us, exhorting us to courage, had but a restricted influence on my mind.

Especially when the orders came for the rolling stock to be dynamited.

For we had brought with us, in our retreat from Magersfontein, practically all the carriages and engines and trucks of the Transvaal and Orange Free State railways. At first we were much saddened by the necessity for destroying the property of our country. But afterwards something got into our blood which made it all seem like a good joke.

I know that our own little group that was under the leadership of Veldkornet Stefanus Malherbe really derived a considerable amount of enjoyment, towards the end, out of blowing railway engines and whole trains into the air. A couple of former shunters who were on commando with us would say things like, "There goes the Cape mail via Fourteen Streams." And we would fling ourselves into a ditch to escape the flying fragments of wood and steel. One of them also used to shout, "All seats for Bloemfontein," or "First stop Elandsfontein," after the fuse was lit and he would blow his whistle and wave a green flag. For several days it seemed that between Nelspruit and Hectorspruit you couldn't look up at any part of the sky without seeing wheels in it.

And during all this time we treated the whole affair as fun, and the former shunters had got to calling out, "There goes the 9.20 to De Aar against the signals," and, "There's a girl with fair hair travelling by herself in the end compartment." Being railwaymen, they couldn't think of anything else to say.

Because the war of the big commandos, and of men like Generals Joubert and Cronje, was over, it seemed to us that all the fighting was just about done. We did not know that the Boer War of General de Wet and Ben Viljoen and General Muller was then only about to begin.

The next order that our veldkornet, Stefanus Malherbe, brought us from the kommandant was for the destruction of our stores and field guns and ammunition dumps as well. All we had to retain were our Mausers and horses, the order said. That did not give us much cause for hope. At the same time the first of General Louis Botha's burghers from the Dalmanutha fight began to arrive in our camp. They were worn out from their long retreat and many of them had acquired the singular habit of looking round over their shoulders very quickly, every so often, right in the middle of a conversation. Their presence did not help to inspire us with military ardour. One of these burghers was very upset at our having blown up all the trains. He had been born and bred in the gramadoelas and had been looking forward to his first journey by rail.

"I just wanted to feel how the thing rides," he said in disappointed tones, in between trying to wipe off stray patches of yellow lyddite stains he had got at Dalmanutha. "But even if there *was* still another train left, I suppose it would be too late, now."

"Yes, I am sure it would be too late," I said, also looking quickly over my shoulder. There was something infectious about this habit that Louis Botha's burghers had brought with them.

Actually, of course, it was not yet too late, for there was still a train, with the engine and carriages intact, waiting to take the president out of the Transvaal into Portuguese territory. There were also in the Boer ranks men whose loyalty to the Republic never wavered even in the darkest times. It had been a very long retreat from the Northern Cape Province through the Orange Free State and the Transvaal to where we were now shut in near the Komati River. And it had all happened so quickly.

The Boer withdrawal, when once it got under way, had been fast and complete. I found it not a little disconcerting to think that on one day I had seen the president seated in a spider just outside Paardeberg drinking buttermilk and then on another day, only a few months later, I had seen him sitting on the front stoep of a house at Waterval Onder a thousand miles away, drinking brandy. Moreover, he was getting ready to move again.

"If it is only to Europe that he is going, then it is not too bad," said an old farmer with a long beard who was an ignorant man in many ways, but whose faith had not faltered throughout the retreat. "I would not have liked our beloved president to have to travel all that way back to the Northern Cape where we started from. He hasn't the strength for so long a journey. I am glad that it is only to Russia that he is going."

Because he was not demoralised by defeat, as so many of us were, we who listened to this old farmer's words were touched by his simple loyalty. Indeed, the example set by men of his sort had a far greater influence on the course of the war during the difficult period ahead than the speeches that our leaders came round and made to us from time to time.

Certainly we did not feel that the veldkornet, Stefanus Malherbe, was a tower of strength. We did not dislike him nor did we distrust him. We only felt, after a peculiar fashion, that he was too much the same kind of man that we ourselves were. So we did not have overmuch respect for him.

I have said that we ordinary burghers did not have the temerity to approach the president and to talk to him as man to man of the matter that we wanted to know about. And so we hung back a little while Stefanus Malherbe, an officer on whom many weighty responsibilities reposed, put out his chest and strode toward the house to interview the president. "Put out your stomach," one of the burghers called out. He was of course thinking of those men who until lately had surrounded the president with their papers and watch-chains and cigars.

And then, when Stefanus Malherbe was moving in the direction of the voorkamer, where he knew the president to be, and when the rest of the members of our veldkornetskap had drawn ourselves together in a little knot that stood nervously waiting just off the stoep for the president's reply – I suppose it had to happen that just then a newly appointed general should have decided to treat us to a patriotic talk. Under other circumstances we would have been impressed, perhaps, but at that point in time, when we had already blown up our trains and stores and ammunition dumps, and had sunk the pieces that remained of the Staat's

Artillerie in the Komati River – along with some papers we had captured in earlier battle – we were not an ideal audience.

We stood still, out of politeness, and listened. But all the time we were wondering if the veldkornet would perhaps be able to slip away at the end of the speech and manage to get in a few words with President Kruger after all. Anyway, I am sure that we took in very little of what the newly appointed general had to say.

In the end the general realised the position too. We gathered that he had known he was going to get the appointment that day, and that he had prepared a speech for the occasion, to deliver before the president and the State Council, but that he had been unable to have his say in the house because of the bustle attendant upon the president's impending departure. Consequently, the general delivered his set speech to us, the first group of burghers he encountered on his way out. After he had got us to sing Psalm 83 and had adjured each one of us to humble himself before the Lord, the general explained at great length that if we could perhaps not hope for victory, since victory might be beyond our capacity, we could still hope for a more worthy kind of defeat.

We made no response to his eloquence. We did not sweep our hats upward in a cheer. We did not call out, "Ou perd!" We were only concerned with the veldkornet's chances of getting in a word with the president before it was too late. The general understood, eventually, that our hearts were not in his address and so he concluded his speech rather abruptly. "Some defeats are greater than victories," he said, and he paused for a little while to survey us before adding, "but not this one, I don't think."

The meeting having ended suddenly like that, Veldkornet Stefanus Malherbe did, after all, manage to get into the voorkamer to speak to President Kruger alone. That much we knew. But when he came out of the house, the veldkornet was silent about his conversation with the president. He did not tell us what the president had said in answer to his question. And in the next advance of the English, which was made within that same week, and which took them right into Komatipoort, Veldkornet Stefanus Malherbe was killed. So he never told us what the president had said in answer to his question about the Kruger millions.

KAREL FLYSMAN

It was after the English had taken Pretoria that I first met Karel Flysman, Oom Schalk Lourens said.

Karel was about twenty-five. He was a very tall, well-built young man with a red face and curly hair. He was good-looking, and while I was satisfied with what the good Lord had done for me, yet I felt sometimes that if only He had given me a body like what Karel Flysman had got, I would go to church oftener and put more in the collection plate.

When the big commandos broke up, we separated into small companies, so that the English would not be able to catch all the Republican forces at the same time. If we were few and scattered the English would have to look harder to find us in the dongas and bushes and rante. And the English, at the beginning, moved slowly. When their scouts saw us making coffee under the trees by the side of the spruit, where it was cool and pleasant, they turned back to the main army and told their general about us. The general would look through his field-glasses and nod his head a few times.

"Yes," he would say, "that is the enemy. I can see them under those trees. There's that man with the long beard eating out of a pot with his hands. Why doesn't he use a knife and fork? I don't think he can be a gentleman. Bring out the maps and we'll attack them."

Then the general and a few of his kommandants would get together and work it all out.

"This cross I put here will be those trees," the general would say. "This crooked line I am drawing here is the spruit, and this circle will stand for the pot that that man is eating out of with his fingers. . . No, that's no good, now. They've moved the pot. Wonderful how crafty these Boers are."

Anyway, they would work out the plans of our position for half an hour, and at the end of that time they would find out that they had got it all wrong. Because they had been using a map of the Rustenburg District, and actually they were halfway into the Marico. So by the time they had everything ready to attack us, we had already moved off and were making coffee under some other trees.

How do I know all these things? Well, I went right through the Boer War, and I was only once caught. And that was when our kommandant, Apie Terblanche, led us through the Bushveld by following some maps that he had captured from the British. But Apie Terblanche never was much use. He couldn't even hang a Hottentot properly.

As I was saying, Karel Flysman first joined up with our commando when we were trekking through the Bushveld north of the railway line from Mafeking to Bulawayo. It seemed that he had got separated from his commando and that he had been wandering about through the bush for some days before he came across us. He was mounted on a big black horse and, as he rode well, even for a Boer, he was certainly the finest-looking burgher I had seen for a long time.

One afternoon, when we had been in the saddle since before sunrise, and had also been riding hard the day before, we off-saddled at the foot of a koppie, where the bush was high and thick. We were very tired. A British column had come across us near the Molopo River. The meeting was a surprise for the British as well as for us. We fought for about an hour, but the fire was so heavy that we had to retreat, leaving behind us close on a dozen men, including the veldkornet. Karel Flysman displayed great promptitude and decision. As soon as the first shot was fired he jumped off his horse and threw down his rifle; he crawled away from the enemy on his hands and knees. He crawled very quickly too. An hour later, when we had ourselves given up resisting the English, we came across him in some long grass about a mile away from where the fighting had been. He was still crawling.

Karel Flysman's horse had remained with the rest of the horses, and it was just by good luck that Karel was able to get into the saddle and take to flight with us before the English got too close. We were pursued for a considerable distance. It didn't seem as though we would ever be able to shake off the enemy. I suppose that the reason they followed us so well was because that column could not have been in charge of a general; their leader must have been only a captain or a kommandant, who probably did not understand how to use a map.

It was towards the afternoon that we discovered that the English were no longer hanging on to our rear. When we dismounted in the thick bush at the foot of the koppie, it was all we could do to unsaddle our horses. Then we lay down on the grass and stretched out our limbs and turned round to get comfortable, but we were so fatigued that it was a long time before we could get into restful positions.

Even then we couldn't get to sleep. The kommandant called us together and selected a number of burghers who were to form a committee to try Karel Flysman for running away. There wasn't much to be said about it. Karel Flysman was young, but at the same time he was old enough to know better. An ordinary burgher has got no right to run away from a fight at the head of the commando. It was the general's place to run away first. As a member of this committee I was at pains to point all this out to the prisoner.

We were seated in a circle on the grass. Karel Flysman stood in the centre. He was bare-headed. His Mauser and bandolier had been taken away from him. His trousers were muddy and broken at the knees from the way in which he had crawled that long distance through the grass. There was also mud on his face. But in spite of all that, there was a fine, manly look about him, and I am sure that others besides myself felt sorry that Karel Flysman should be so much of a coward.

We were sorry for him, in a way. We were also tired, so that we didn't feel like getting up and doing any more shooting. Accordingly we decided that if the kommandant warned him about it we would give him one more chance.

"You have heard what your fellow-burghers have decided about you," the kommandant said. "Let this be a lesson to you. A burgher of the Republic who runs away quickly may rise to be kommandant. But a burgher of the Republic must also know that there is a time to fight. And it is better to be shot by the English than by your own people, even though," the kommandant added, "the English can't shoot straight."

So we gave Karel Flysman back his rifle and bandolier, and we went to sleep. We didn't even trouble to put out guards round the camp. It would not have been any use putting out pickets, for they would have been sure to fall asleep, and if the English did come during the night they would know of our whereabouts by falling over the pickets.

As it happened, that night the English came.

The first thing I knew about it was when a man put his foot on my face. He put it on heavily, too, and by the feel of it I could tell that his veldskoens were made of unusually hard ox-hide. In those days, through always being on the alert for the enemy, I was a light sleeper, and that man's boot on my face woke me up without any difficulty. In the darkness I swore at him and he cursed back at me, saying something about the English. So we carried on for a few moments; he spoke about the English; I spoke about my face.

Then I heard the kommandant's voice, shouting out orders for us to stand to arms. I got my rifle and found my way to a sloot where our men were gathering for the fight. Up to that moment it had been too dark for me to distinguish anything that was more than a few feet away from me. But just then the clouds drifted away, and the moon shone down on us. It happened so quickly that for a brief while I was almost afraid. Everything that had been black before suddenly stood out pale and ghostly. The trees became silver with dark shadows in them, and it was amongst these shadows that we strove to see the English. Wherever a branch rustled in the wind or a twig moved, we thought we could see soldiers. Then somebody fired a shot. At once the firing became general.

I had been in many fights before, so that there was nothing new to me in the rattle of Mausers and Lee-Metfords, and in the red spurts of flame that suddenly broke out all round us. We could see little of the English. That meant that they could see even less of us. All we had to aim at were those spurts of flame. We realised quickly that it was only an advance party of the English that we had up against us; it was all rifle fire; the artillery would be coming along behind the main body. What we had to do was to go on shooting a little longer and then slip away before the rest of the English came. Near me a man shouted that he was hit. Many more were hit that night.

I bent down to put another cartridge-clip into my magazine, when I noticed a man lying flat in the sloot, with his arms about his head. His gun lay on the grass in front of him. By his dress and the size of his body I knew it was Karel Flysman. I didn't know whether it was a bullet or cowardice that had brought him down in that way. Therefore, to find out, I trod on his face. He shouted out something about the English, whereupon (as he used the same words), I was satisfied that he was the man who had awakened me with his boot before the fight started. I put some more of my weight on to the foot that was on his face.

"Don't do that. Oh, don't," Karel Flysman shouted. "I am dying. Oh, I am sure I am dying. The English. . . "

I stooped down and examined him. He was unwounded. All that was wrong with him was his spirit.

"God," I said, "why can't you try to be a man, Karel? If you've got to be shot nothing can stop the bullet, whether you are afraid or whether you're not. To see the way you're lying down there anybody would think that you are at least the kommandant-general."

He blurted out a lot of things, but he spoke so rapidly and his lips trembled so much that I couldn't understand much of what he said. And I didn't want to understand him, either. I kicked him in the ribs and told him to take his rifle and fight, or I would shoot him as he lay. But of course all that was of no use. He was actually so afraid of the enemy that even if he knew for sure that I was going to shoot him he would just have lain down where he was and have waited for the bullet.

In the meantime the fire of the enemy had grown steadier, so that we knew that at any moment we could expect the order to retreat.

"In a few minutes you can get back to your old game of running," I shouted to Karel Flysman, but I don't think he heard much of what I said, on account of the continuous rattle of the rifles.

But he must have heard the word "running".

"I can't," he cried. "My legs are too weak. I am dying."

He went on like that some more. He also mentioned a girl's name. He repeated it several times. I think the name was Francina. He shouted out the name and cried out that he didn't want to die. Then a whistle blew, and shortly afterwards we got the order to prepare for the retreat.

I did my best to help Karel out of the sloot. The Englishmen would have laughed if they could have seen that struggle in the moonlight. But the affair didn't last too long. Karel suddenly collapsed back into the sloot and lay still. That time it was a bullet. Karel Flysman was dead.

Often after I have thought of Karel Flysman and of the way he died. I have also thought of that girl he spoke about. Perhaps she thinks of her lover as a hero who laid down his life for his country. And perhaps it is as well that she should think that.

THE TRAITOR'S WIFE

We did not like the sound of the wind that morning, as we cantered over a veld trail that we had made much use of, during the past year, when there were English forces in the neighbourhood.

The wind blew short wisps of yellow grass in quick flurries over the veld and the smoke from the fire in front of a row of kaffir huts hung low in the air. From that we knew that the third winter of the Boer War was at hand. Our small group of burghers dismounted at the edge of a clump of camel-thorns to rest our horses.

"It's going to be an early winter," Jan Vermeulen said, and from force of habit he put his hand up to his throat in order to close his jacket collar over in front. We all laughed, then. We realised that Jan Vermeulen had forgotten how he had come to leave his jacket behind when the English had surprised us at the spruit a few days before. And instead of a jacket, he was now wearing a mealie sack with holes cut in it for his head and arms. You could not just close over in front of your throat, airily, the lapels cut in a grain bag.

"Anyway, Jan, you're all right for clothes," Kobus Ferreira said, "but look at me."

Kobus Ferreira was wearing a missionary's frock-coat that he had found outside Kronendal, where it had been hung on a clothes-line to air.

"This frock-coat is cut so tight across my middle and shoulders that I have to sit very stiff and awkward in my saddle, just like the missionary sits on a chair when he is visiting at a farmhouse," Kobus Ferreira added. "Several times my horse has taken me for an Englishman, in consequence of the way I sit. I am only afraid that when a bugle blows my horse will carry me over the rant into the English camp."

At Kobus Ferreira's remark the early winter wind seemed to take on a keener edge.

For our thoughts went immediately to Leendert Roux, who had been with us on commando a long while and who had been spoken of as a likely man to be veldkornet – and who had gone scouting, one night, and did not come back with a report.

There were, of course, other Boers who had also joined the English. But there was not one of them that we had respected as much as we had done Leendert Roux.

Shortly afterwards we were on the move again.

In the late afternoon we emerged through the Crocodile Poort that brought us in sight of Leendert Roux's farmhouse. Next to the dam was a patch of mealies that Leendert Roux's wife had got the kaffirs to cultivate.

"Anyway, we'll camp on Leendert Roux's farm and eat roast mealies tonight," our veldkornet, Apie Theron, observed.

"Let us first rather burn his house down," Kobus Ferreira said. And in a strange way it seemed as though his violent language was not out of place in a missionary's frock-coat. "I would like to roast mealies in the thatch of Leendert Roux's house."

Many of us were in agreement with Kobus.

But our veldkornet, Apie Theron, counselled us against that form of vengeance.

"Leendert Roux's having his wife and farmstead here will yet lead to his undoing," the veldkornet said. "One day he will risk coming out here on a visit, when he hasn't got Kitchener's whole army at his back. That will be when we will settle our reckoning with him."

We did not guess that that day would be soon.

The road we were following led past Leendert Roux's homestead. The noise of our horses' hooves brought Leendert Roux's wife, Serfina, to the door. She stood in the open doorway and watched us riding by. Serfina was pretty, taller than most women, and slender, and there was no expression in her eyes that you could read, and her face was very white.

It was strange, I thought, as we rode past the homestead, that the sight of Serfina Roux did not fill us with bitterness.

Afterwards, when we had dismounted in the mealie-land, Jan Vermeulen made a remark at which we laughed.

"For me it was the worst moment in the Boer War," Jan Vermeulen said. "Having to ride past a pretty girl, and me wearing just a sack. I was glad there was Kobus Ferreira's frock-coat for me to hide behind."

Jurie Bekker said there was something about Serfina Roux that reminded him of the Transvaal. He did not know how it was, but he repeated that, with the wind of early winter fluttering her dresses about her ankles, that was how it seemed to him.

Then Kobus Ferreira said that he had wanted to shout out something to her when we rode past the door, to let Serfina know how we, who were fighting in the last ditch – and in unsuitable clothing – felt about the wife of a traitor. "But she stood there so still," Kobus Ferreira said, "that I just couldn't say anything. I felt I would like to visit her, even."

That remark of Kobus Ferreira's fitted in with his frock-coat, also. It would not be the first time a man in ecclesiastical dress called on a woman while her husband was away.

Then, once again, a remark of Jan Vermeulen's made us realise that there was a war on. Jan Vermeulen had taken the mealie sack off his body and had threaded a length of baling-wire above the places where the holes were. He was now restoring the grain bag to the use it had been meant for, and I suppose that, in consequence, his views generally also got sensible.

"Just because Serfina Roux is pretty," Jan Vermeulen said, flinging mealie heads into the sack, "let us not forget who and what she is. Perhaps it is not safe for us to camp tonight on this farm. She is sure to be in touch with the English. She may tell them where we are. Especially now that we have taken her mealies."

But our veldkornet said that it wasn't important if the English knew where we were. Indeed, any kaffir in the neighbourhood could go and report our position to them. But what did matter was that we should know where the English were. And he reminded us that in two years he had never made a serious mistake that way.

"What about the affair at the spruit, though?" Jan Vermeulen asked him. "And my pipe and tinder-box were in the jacket, too."

By sunset the wind had gone down. But there was a chill in the air. We had pitched our camp in the tamboekie grass on the far side of Leendert Roux's farm. And I was glad, lying in my blankets, to think that it was the turn of the veldkornet and Jurie Bekker to stand guard.

Far away a jackal howled. Then there was silence again. A little later the stillness was disturbed by sterner sounds of the veld at night. And those sounds did not come from very far away, either. They were sounds Jurie Bekker made – first, when he fell over a beacon, and then when he gave his opinion of Leendert Roux for setting up a beacon in the middle of a stretch of dubbeltjie thorns. The blankets felt very snug, pulled over my shoulders, when I reflected on those thorns.

And because I was young, there came into my thoughts, at Jurie Bekker's mention of Leendert Roux, the picture of Serfina as she had stood in front of her door.

The dream I had of Serfina Roux was that she came to me, tall and graceful, beside a white beacon on her husband's farm. It was that haunting kind of dream, in which you half know all the time that you are dreaming. And she was very beautiful in my dream. And it was as though her hair was hanging half out of my dream and reaching down into the wind when she came closer to me. And I knew what she wanted to tell me. But I did not wish to hear it. I knew that if Serfina spoke that thing I would wake up from my dream. And, in that moment, like it always happens in a dream, Serfina did speak.

"Opskud, kêrels!" I heard.

But it was not Serfina who gave that command. It was Apie Theron, the veldkornet. He came running into the camp with his rifle at the trail. And Serfina was gone. In a few minutes we had saddled our horses and were ready to gallop away. Many times during the past couple of years our scouts had roused us thus when an English column was approaching.

We were already in the saddle when Apie Theron let us know what was toward. He had received information, he said, that Leendert Roux had that very night ventured back to his homestead. If we hurried we might trap him in his own house. The veldkornet warned us to take no chances, reminding us that when Leendert Roux had still stood on our side he had been a fearless and resourceful fighter.

So we rode back during the night along the same way we had come in the afternoon. We tethered our horses in a clump of trees near the mealie-land and started to surround the farmhouse. When we saw a figure running for the stable at the side of the house, we realised that Leendert Roux had been almost too quick for us.

In the cold, thin wind that springs up just before the dawn we surprised Leendert Roux at the door of his stable. But when he made no resistance it was almost as though it was Leendert Roux who had taken us by surprise. Leendert Roux's calm acceptance of his fate made it seem almost as though he had never turned traitor, but that he was laying down his life for the Transvaal.

In answer to the veldkornet's question, Leendert Roux said that he would be glad if Kobus Ferreira – he having noticed that Kobus was wearing the frock-coat of a man of religion – would read Psalm 110 over his grave. He also said that he did not want his eyes bandaged. And he asked to be allowed to say goodbye to his wife.

Serfina was sent for. At the side of the stable, in the wind of early morning, Leendert and Serfina Roux, husband and wife, bade each other farewell.

Serfina looked even more shadowy than she had done in my dream when she set off back to the homestead along the footpath through the thorns. The sun was just beginning to rise. And I understood how right Jurie Bekker had been when he said that she was just like the Transvaal, with the dawn wind fluttering her skirts about her ankles as it rippled the grass. And I remembered that it was the Boer women that kept on when their menfolk recoiled before the steepness of the Drakensberge and spoke of turning back.

I also thought of how strange it was that Serfina should have come walking over to our camp, in the middle of the night, just as she had done in my dream. But where my dream was different was that she had reported not to me but to our veldkornet where Leendert Roux was.

PEACHES RIPENING
IN THE SUN

The way Ben Myburg lost his memory (Oom Schalk Lourens said) made a deep impression on all of us. We reasoned that that was the sort of thing that a sudden shock could do to you. There were those in our small section of General du Toit's commando who could recall similar stories of how people in a moment could forget everything about the past, just because of a single dreadful happening.

A shock like that can have the same effect on you even if you are prepared for it. Maybe it can be worse, even. And in this connection I often think of what it says in the Good Book, about that which you most feared having now at last caught up with you.

Our commando went as far as the border by train. And when the engine came to a stop on a piece of open veld, and it wasn't for water, this time, and the engine-driver and fireman didn't step down with a spanner and use bad language, then we understood that the train stopping there was the beginning of the Second Boer War.

We were wearing new clothes and we had new equipment, and the sun was shining on the barrels of our Mausers. Our new clothes had been requisitioned for us by our veldkornet at stores along the way. All the veldkornet had to do was to sign his name on a piece of paper for whatever his men purchased.

In most cases, after we had patronised a store in that manner, the shopkeeper would put up his shutters for the day. And three years would pass and the Boer War would be over before the shopkeeper would display any sort of inclination to take the shutters down again.

Maybe he should have put them up before we came.

Only one 'seksie' of General du Toit's commando entered Natal looking considerably dilapidated. This 'seksie' looked as though it was already the end of the Boer War, and not just the beginning. Afterwards we found out that their veldkornet had never learnt to write his name. We were glad that in the first big battle these men kept well to the rear, apparently conscious of how sinful they looked. For, to make matters worse, a regiment of Indian troops was fighting on that front, and we were not anxious that an Eastern race should see white men at such a disadvantage.

"You don't seem to remember me, Schalk," a young fellow came up and said to me. I admitted that I didn't recognise him, straight away, as Ben Myburg. He did look different in those smart light-green riding pants and that new hat with the ostrich feather stuck in it. You could see that he had patronised some mine concession store before the owner got his shutters down.

"But I would know you anywhere, Schalk," Ben Myburg went on. "Just from the quick way you hid that soap under your saddle a couple of minutes ago. I remembered where I had last seen something so quick. It was two years ago, at the Nagmaal in Nylstroom."

I told Ben Myburg that if it was that jar of brandy he meant, then he must realise that there had also been a good deal of misunderstanding about it. Moreover, it was not even a full jar, I said.

But I congratulated him on his powers of memory, which I said I was sure would yet stand the Republic in good stead.

And I was right. For afterwards, when the war of the big commandos was over, and we were in constant retreat, it would be Ben Myburg who, next day, would lead us back to the donga in which we had hidden some mealie-meal and a tin of cooking fat. And if the tin of cooking fat was empty, he would be able to tell us right away if it was kaffirs or baboons. A kaffir had a different way of eating cooking fat out of a tin from what a baboon had, Ben Myburg said.

Ben Myburg had been recently married to Mimi van Blerk, who came from Schweizer-Reneke, a district that was known as far as the Limpopo for its attractive girls. I remembered Mimi van Blerk well. She had full red lips and thick yellow hair. Ben Myburgh always looked forward very eagerly to getting letters from his pretty young wife. He would also read out to us extracts from her letters, in which she encouraged us to drive the English into the blue grass – which was the name we gave to the sea in those days. For the English we had other names.

One of Mimi's letters was accompanied by a wooden candle-box filled with dried peaches. Ben Myburg was most proud to share out the dried fruit among our company, for he had several times spoken of the orchard of yellow cling peaches that he had laid out at the side of his house.

"We've already got dried peaches," Jurie Bekker said. Then he added, making free with our projected invasion of Natal: "In a few weeks' time we will be picking bananas."

It was in this spirit, as I have said, that we set out to meet the enemy. But nobody knew better than ourselves how much of this fine talk was to hide what we really felt. And I know, speaking for myself, that when we got the command "Opsaal", and we were crossing the border between the Transvaal and Natal, I was less happy at the thought that my horse was such a mettlesome animal. For it seemed to me that my horse was far more anxious to invade Natal than I was. I had to rein him in a good deal on the way to Spioenkop and Colenso. And I told myself that it was because I did not want him to go too fast downhill.

Eighteen months later saw the armed forces of the Republic in a worse case than I should imagine any army has ever been in, and that army still fighting. We were spread all over the country in small groups. We were in rags.

Many burghers had been taken prisoner. Others had yielded themselves up to British magistrates, holding not their rifles in their hands but their hats. There were a number of Boers, also, who had gone and joined the English.

For the Transvaal Republic it was near the end of a tale that you tell, sitting around the kitchen fire on a cold night. The story of the Transvaal Republic was at that place where you clear your throat before saying which of the two men the girl finally married. Or whether it was the cattle smuggler or the Sunday school superintendent who stole the money. Or whether it was a real ghost or just her uncle with a sheet round him that Lettie van Zyl saw at the drift.

One night, when we were camped just outside Nietverdiend, and it was Ben Myburg's and my turn to go on guard, he told me that he knew that part well.

"You see that rant there, Schalk?" he asked. "Well, I have often stood on the other side of it, under the stars, just like now. You know, I've got a lot of peach-trees on my farm. Well, I have stood there, under the ripening peaches, just after dark, with Mimi at my side. There is no smell like the smell of young peach-trees in the evening, Schalk, when the fruit is ripening. I can almost imagine I am back there now. And it is just the time for it, too."

I tried to explain to Ben Myburg, in a roundabout way, that although everything might be exactly the same on this side of the rant, he would have to be prepared for certain changes on the other side, seeing that it was war.

Ben Myburg agreed that I was probably right. Nevertheless, he began to talk to me at length about his courtship days. He spoke of Mimi with her full red lips and her yellow hair.

"I can still remember the evening when Mimi promised that she would marry me, Schalk," Ben Myburg said. "It was in Zeerust. We were there for the Nagmaal. When I walked back to my tent on the kerkplein I was so happy that I just kicked the first three kaffirs I saw."

I could see that, talking to me while we stood on guard, Ben Myburg was living through that time all over again. I was glad, for their sakes, that no kaffirs came past at that moment. For Ben Myburg was again very happy.

I was pleased, too, for Ben Myburg's own sake, that he did at least have that hour of deep joy in which he could recall the past so vividly. For it was after that that his memory went.

By the following evening we had crossed the rant and had arrived at Ben Myburg's farm. We camped among the smoke-blackened walls of his former homestead, erecting a rough shelter with some sheets of corrugated iron that we could still use. And although he must have known only too well what to expect, yet what Ben Myburg saw there came as so much of a shock to his senses that from that moment all he could remember from the past vanished for ever.

It was pitiful to see the change that had come over him. If his farm had been laid to ruins, the devastation that had taken place in Ben Myburg's mind was no less dreadful.

Perhaps it was that, in truth, there was nothing more left in the past to remember.

We noticed, also, that in singular ways, certain fragments of the by-gone would come into Ben Myburg's mind; and that he would almost – but not quite – succeed in fitting these pieces together.

We observed that almost immediately. For instance, we remained camped on his farm for several days. And one morning, when the fire for our mealie-pap was crackling under one of the few remaining fruit-trees that had once been an orchard, Ben Myburg reached up and picked a peach that was, in advance of its season, ripe and yellow.

"It's funny," Ben Myburg said, "but I seem to remember, from long ago, reaching up and picking a yellow peach, just like this one. I don't quite remember where."

We did not tell him that he was picking one of his own peaches.

Some time later our 'seksie' was captured in a night attack.

For us the Boer War was over. We were going to St. Helena. We were driven to Nylstroom, the nearest railhead, in a mule-wagon. It was a strange experience for us to be driving along the main road, in broad daylight, for all the world to see us. From years of war-time habit, our eyes still went to the horizon. A bitter thing about our captivity was that among our guards were men of our own people.

Outside Nylstroom we alighted from the mule-wagon and the English sergeant in charge of our escort got us to form fours by the roadside. It was queer – our having to learn to be soldiers at the end of a war instead of at the beginning.

Eventually we got into some sort of formation, the veldkornet, Jurie Bekker, Ben Myburg and I making up the first four. It was already evening. From a distance we could see the lights in the town. The way to the main street of Nylstroom led by the cemetery. Although it was dark, we could yet distinguish several rows of newly made mounds. We did not need to be told that they were concentration camp graves. We took off our battered hats and tramped on in great silence.

Soon we were in the main street. We saw, then, what those lights were. There was a dance at the hotel. Paraffin lamps were hanging under the hotel's low, wide verandah. There was much laughter. We saw girls and English officers. In our unaccustomed fours we slouched past in the dark.

Several of the girls went inside, then. But a few of the womenfolk remained on the verandah, not looking in our direction. Among them I noticed particularly a girl leaning on an English officer's shoulder. She looked very pretty, with the light from a paraffin lamp shining on her full lips and yellow hair.

When we had turned the corner, and the darkness was wrapping us round again, I heard Ben Myburg speak.

"It's funny," I heard Ben Myburg say, "but I seem to remember, from long ago, a girl with yellow hair, just like that one. I don't quite remember where."

And this time, too, we did not tell him.

THE ROOINEK

Rooineks, said Oom Schalk Lourens, are queer. For instance, there was that day when my nephew Hannes and I had dealings with a couple of Englishmen near Dewetsdorp. It was shortly after Sanna's Post, and Hannes and I were lying behind a rock watching the road. Hannes spent odd moments like that in what he called a useful way. He would file the points of his Mauser cartridges on a piece of flat stone until the lead showed through the steel, in that way making them into dum-dum bullets.

I often spoke to my nephew Hannes about that.

"Hannes," I used to say. "That is a sin. The Lord is looking at you."

"That's all right," Hannes replied. "The Lord knows that this is the Boer War, and in war-time he will always forgive a little foolishness like this, especially as the English are so many."

Anyway, as we lay behind that rock we saw, far down the road, two horsemen come galloping up. We remained perfectly still and let them approach to within four hundred paces. They were English officers. They were mounted on first-rate horses and their uniforms looked very fine and smart. They were the most stylish-looking men I had seen for some time, and I felt quite ashamed of my own ragged trousers and veldskoens. I was glad that I was behind a rock and they couldn't see me. Especially as my jacket was also torn all the way down the back, as a result of my having had, three days before, to get through a barbed-wire fence rather quickly. I just got through in time, too. The veldkornet, who was a fat man and couldn't run so fast, was about twenty yards behind me. And he remained on the wire with a bullet through him. All through the Boer War I was pleased that I was thin and never troubled with corns.

Hannes and I fired just about the same time. One of the officers fell off his horse. He struck the road with his shoulders and rolled over twice, kicking up the red dust as he turned. Then the other soldier did a queer thing. He drew up his horse and got off. He gave just one look in our direction. Then he led his horse up to where the other man was twisting and struggling on the ground. It took him a little while to lift him on to his horse, for it is no easy matter to pick up a man like that when he is helpless. And he did all this slowly and calmly, as though he was not concerned about the fact that the men who had shot his friend were lying only a few hundred yards away. He managed in some way to support the wounded man across the saddle, and walked on beside the horse. After going a few yards he stopped and seemed to remember something. He turned round and waved at the spot where he imagined we were hiding, as though inviting us to shoot. During all that time I had simply lain watching him, astonished at his coolness.

But when he waved his hand I thrust another cartridge into the breach of my Martini and aimed. At that distance I couldn't miss. I aimed very carefully and was just on the point of pulling the trigger when Hannes put his hand on the barrel and pushed up my rifle.

"Don't shoot, Oom Schalk," he said. "That's a brave man."

I looked at Hannes in surprise. His face was very white. I said nothing, and allowed my rifle to sink down on to the grass, but I couldn't understand what had come over my nephew. It seemed that not only was that Englishman queer, but that Hannes was also queer. That's all nonsense not killing a man just because he's brave. If he's a brave man and he's fighting on the wrong side, that's all the more reason to shoot him.

I was with my nephew Hannes for another few months after that. Then one day, in a skirmish near the Vaal River, Hannes with a few dozen other burghers was cut off from the commando and had to surrender. That was the last I ever saw of him. I heard later on that, after taking him prisoner, the English searched Hannes and found dum-dum bullets in his possession. They shot him for that. I was very much grieved when I heard of Hannes's death. He had always been full of life and high spirits. Perhaps Hannes was right in saying that the Lord didn't mind about a little foolishness like dum-dum bullets. But the mistake he made was in forgetting that the English did mind.

I was in the veld until they made peace. Then we laid down our rifles and went home. What I knew my farm by was the hole under the koppie where I quarried slate-stones for the threshing-floor. That was about all that remained as I left it. Everything else was gone. My home was burnt down. My lands were laid waste. My cattle and sheep were slaughtered. Even the stones I had piled for the kraals were pulled down. My wife came out of the concentration camp, and we went together to look at our old farm. My wife had gone into the concentration camp with our two children, but she came out alone. And when I saw her again and noticed the way she had changed, I knew that I, who had been through all the fighting, had not seen the Boer War.

Neither Sannie nor I had the heart to go on farming again on that same place. It would be different without the children playing about the house and getting into mischief. We got paid out some money by the new Government for part of our losses. So I bought a wagon and oxen and left the Free State, which was not even the Free State any longer. It was now called the Orange River Colony.

We trekked right through the Transvaal into the northern part of the Marico Bushveld. Years ago, as a boy, I had trekked through that same country with my parents. Now that I went there again I felt that it was still a good country. It was on the far side of the Dwarsberge, near Derdepoort, that we got a Government farm. Afterwards other farmers trekked in there as well. One or two of them had also come from the Free State, and I knew them. There were also a few Cape rebels whom I had seen on commando. All of us had lost relatives in the war. Some had died in the concentration camps or on the battlefield. Others had been shot for going into rebellion. So, taken all in all, we who had trekked into that part of the Marico that lay nearest the Bechuanaland border were very bitter against the English.

Then it was that the rooinek came.

It was in the first year of our having settled around Derdepoort. We heard that an Englishman had bought a farm next to Gerhardus Grobbelaar. This was when we were sitting in the voorkamer of Willem Odendaal's house, which was used as a post office. Once a week the post-cart came up with letters from Zeerust, and we came together at Willem Odendaal's house and talked and smoked and drank coffee. Very few of us ever got letters, and then it was mostly demands to pay for the boreholes that had been drilled on our farms or for cement and fencing materials. But every week regularly we went for the post. Sometimes the post-cart didn't come, because the Groen River was in flood, and we would most of us have gone home without noticing it, if somebody didn't speak about it.

When Koos Steyn heard that an Englishman was coming to live amongst us he got up from the riempies-bank.

"No, kêrels," he said. "Always when the Englishman comes, it means that a little later the Boer has got to shift. I'll pack up my wagon and make coffee, and just trek first thing tomorrow morning."

Most of us laughed then. Koos Steyn often said funny things like that. But some didn't laugh. Somehow, there seemed to be too much truth in Koos Steyn's words.

We discussed the matter and decided that if we Boers in the Marico could help it the rooinek would not stay amongst us too long. About half an hour later one of Willem Odendaal's children came in and said that there was a strange wagon coming along the big road. We went to the door and looked out. As the wagon came nearer we saw that it was piled up with all kinds of furniture and also sheets of iron and farming implements. There was so much stuff on the wagon that the tent had to be taken off to get everything on.

The wagon rolled along and came to a stop in front of the house. With the wagon there were one white man and two kaffirs. The white man shouted something to the kaffirs and threw down the whip. Then he walked up to where we were standing. He was dressed just as we were, in shirt and trousers and veldskoens, and he had dust all over him. But when he stepped over a thorn-bush we saw that he had got socks on. Therefore we knew that he was an Englishman.

Koos Steyn was standing in front of the door.

The Englishman went up to him and held out his hand.

"Good afternoon," he said in Afrikaans. "My name is Webber."

Koos shook hands with him.

"My name is Prince Lord Alfred Milner," Koos Steyn said.

That was when Lord Milner was Governor of the Transvaal, and we all laughed. The rooinek also laughed.

"Well, Lord Prince," he said, "I can speak your language a little, and

I hope that later on I'll be able to speak it better. I'm coming to live here, and I hope that we'll all be friends."

He then came round to all of us, but the others turned away and refused to shake hands with him. He came up to me last of all; I felt sorry for him, and although his nation had dealt unjustly with my nation, and I had lost both my children in the concentration camp, still it was not so much the fault of this Englishman. It was the fault of the English Government, who wanted our gold mines. And it was also the fault of Queen Victoria, who didn't like Oom Paul Kruger, because they say that when he went over to London Oom Paul spoke to her only once for a few minutes. Oom Paul Kruger said that he was a married man and he was afraid of widows.

When the Englishman Webber went back to his wagon Koos Steyn and I walked with him. He told us that he had bought the farm next to Gerhardus Grobbelaar and that he didn't know much about sheep and cattle and mealies, but he had bought a few books on farming, and he was going to learn all he could out of them. When he said that I looked away towards the poort. I didn't want him to see that I was laughing. But with Koos Steyn it was otherwise.

"Man," he said, "let me see those books."

Webber opened the box at the bottom of the wagon and took out about six big books with green covers.

"These are very good books," Koos Steyn said. "Yes, they are very good for the white ants. The white ants will eat them all in two nights."

As I have told you, Koos Steyn was a funny fellow, and no man could help laughing at the things he said.

Those were bad times. There was drought, and we could not sow mealies. The dams dried up, and there was only last year's grass on the veld. We had to pump water out of the borehole for weeks at a time. Then the rains came and for a while things were better.

Now and again I saw Webber. From what I heard about him it seemed that he was working hard. But of course no rooinek can make a living out of farming, unless they send him money every month from England. And we found out that almost all the money Webber had was what he had paid on the farm. He was always reading in those green books what he had to do. It's lucky that those books are written in English, and that the Boers can't read them. Otherwise many more farmers would be ruined every year. When his cattle had the heart-water, or his sheep had the blue-tongue, or there were cut-worms or stalk-borers in his mealies, Webber would look it all up in his books. I suppose that when the kaffirs stole his sheep he would look that up too.

Still, Koos Steyn helped Webber quite a lot and taught him a number of things, so that matters did not go as badly with him as they would have if he had only acted according to the lies that were printed in those green books. Webber and Koos Steyn became very friendly. Koos Steyn's wife had had a baby just a few weeks before Webber came. It was the first child they had after being married seven years, and they were very proud of it. It was a girl. Koos Steyn said that he would sooner it had been a boy; but that, even so, it was better than nothing. Right from the first Webber had taken a liking to that child, who was christened Jemima after her mother. Often when I passed Koos Steyn's house I saw the English-man sitting on the front stoep with the child on his knees.

In the meantime the other farmers around there became annoyed on account of Koos Steyn's friendship with the rooinek. They said that Koos was a hendsopper and a traitor to his country. He was intimate with a man who had helped to bring about the downfall of the Afrikaner nation. Yet it was not fair to call Koos a hendsopper. Koos had lived in the Graaff-Reinet District when the war broke out, so that he was a Cape Boer and need not have fought. Nevertheless, he joined up with a Free State commando and remained until peace was made, and if at any time the English had caught him they would have shot him as a rebel, in the same way that they shot Scheepers and many others.

Gerhardus Grobbelaar spoke about this once when we were in Willem Odendaal's post office.

"You are not doing right," Gerhardus said; "Boer and Englishman have been enemies since before Slagtersnek. We've lost this war, but some day we'll win. It's the duty we owe to our children's children to stand against the rooineks. Remember the concentration camps."

There seemed to me to be truth in what Gerhardus said.

"But the English are here now, and we've got to live with them," Koos answered. "When we get to understand one another perhaps we won't need to fight any more. This Englishman Webber is learning Afrikaans very well, and some day he might almost be one of us. The only thing I can't understand about him is that he has a bath every morning. But if he stops that and if he doesn't brush his teeth any more you will hardly be able to tell him from a Boer."

Although he made a joke about it, I felt that in what Koos Steyn said there was also truth.

Then, the year after the drought, the miltsiek broke out. The miltsiek seemed to be in the grass of the veld, and in the water of the dams, and even in the air the cattle breathed. All over the place I would find cows and oxen lying dead. We all became very discouraged. Nearly all of us in that part of the Marico had started farming again on what the Government had given us. Now that the stock died we had nothing. First the drought had put us back to where we were when we started. Now with the miltsiek we couldn't hope to do anything. We couldn't even sow mealies, because, at the rate at which the cattle were dying, in a short while we would have no oxen left to pull the plough. People talked of selling what they had and going to look for work on the gold mines. We sent a petition to the Government, but that did no good.

It was then that somebody got hold of the idea of trekking. In a few days we were talking of nothing else. But the question was where we could trek to. They would not allow us into Rhodesia for fear we might spread the miltsiek there as well. And it was useless going to any other part of the Transvaal. Somebody mentioned German West Africa. We had none of us been there before, and I suppose that really was the reason why, in the end, we decided to go there.

"The blight of the English is over South Africa," Gerhardus Grobbelaar said. "We'll remain here only to die. We most go away somewhere where there is not the Englishman's flag."

In a few weeks' time we arranged everything. We were going to trek across the Kalahari into German territory. Everything we had we loaded up. We drove the cattle ahead and followed behind on our wagons. There were five families: the Steyns, the Grobbelaars, the Odendaals, the Ferreiras and Sannie and I. Webber also came with us. I think it was not so much that he was anxious to leave as that he and Koos Steyn had become very much attached to one another, and the Englishman did not wish to remain alone behind.

The youngest person in our trek was Koos Steyn's daughter Jemima, who was then about eighteen months old. Being the baby, she was a favourite with all of us.

Webber sold his wagon and went with Koos Steyn's trek.

When at the end of the first day we outspanned several miles inside the Bechuanaland Protectorate, we were very pleased that we were done with the Transvaal, where we had had so much misfortune. Of course, the Protectorate was also British territory, but all the same we felt happier there than we had done in our country. We saw Webber every day now, and although he was a foreigner with strange ways, and would remain an Uitlander until he died, yet we disliked him less than before for being a rooinek.

It was on the first Sunday that we reached Malopolole. For the first part of our way the country remained Bushveld. There were the same kind of thorn-trees that grew in the Marico, except that they became fewer the deeper into the Kalahari that we went. Also, the ground became more and more sandy, until even before we came to Malopolole it was all desert. But scattered thorn-bushes remained all the way. That Sunday we held a religious service. Gerhardus Grobbelaar read a chapter out of the Bible and offered up a prayer. We sang a number of psalms, after which Gerhardus prayed again. I shall always remember that Sunday and the way we sat on the ground beside one of the wagons, listening to Gerhardus. That was the last Sunday that we were all together.

The Englishman sat next to Koos Steyn and the baby Jemima lay down in front of him. She played with Webber's fingers and tried to bite them. It was funny to watch her. Several times Webber looked down at her and smiled. I thought then that although Webber was not one of us, yet Jemima certainly did not know it. Maybe in a thing like that the child was wiser than we were. To her it made no difference that the man whose fingers she bit was born in another country and did not speak the same language that she did.

There are many things that I remember about that trek into the

Kalahari. But one thing that now seems strange to me is the way in which, right from the first day, we took Gerhardus Grobbelaar for our leader. Whatever he said we just seemed to do without talking very much about it. We all felt that it was right simply because Gerhardus wished it. That was a strange thing about our trek. It was not simply that we knew Gerhardus had got the Lord with him – for we did know that – but it was rather that we believed in Gerhardus as well as in the Lord. I think that even if Gerhardus Grobbelaar had been an ungodly man we would still have followed him in exactly the same way. For when you are in the desert and there is no water and the way back is long, then you feel that it is better to have with you a strong man who does not read the Book very much, than a man who is good and religious, and yet does not seem sure how far to trek each day and where to outspan.

But Gerhardus Grobbelaar was a man of God. At the same time there was something about him that made you feel that it was only by acting as he advised that you could succeed. There was only one other man I have ever known who found it so easy to get people to do as he wanted. And that was Paul Kruger. He was very much like Gerhardus Grobbelaar, except that Gerhardus was less quarrelsome. But of the two Paul Kruger was the bigger man.

Only once do I remember Gerhardus losing his temper. And that was with the Nagmaal at Elandsberg. It was on a Sunday, and we were camped out beside the Crocodile River. Gerhardus went round early in the morning from wagon to wagon and told us that he wanted everybody to come over to where his wagon stood. The Lord had been good to us at that time, so that we had had much rain and our cattle were fat. Gerhardus explained that he wanted to hold a service, to thank the Lord for all His good works, but more especially for what He had done for the farmers of the northern part of the Groot Marico District. This was a good plan, and we all came together with our Bibles and hymn-books. But one man, Karel Pieterse, remained behind at his wagon. Twice Gerhardus went to call him, but Karel Pieterse lay down on the grass and would not get up to come to the service. He said it was all right thanking the Lord now that there had been rains, but what about all those seasons when there had been drought and the cattle had died of thirst. Gerhardus Grobbelaar shook his head sadly, and said there was nothing he could do then, as it was Sunday. But he prayed that the Lord would soften Brother Pieterse's heart, and he finished off his prayer by saying that in any case, in the morning, he would help to soften the brother's heart himself.

The following morning Gerhardus walked over with a sjambok and an ox-riem to where Karel Pieterse sat before his fire, watching the kaffir making coffee. They were both of them men who were big in the body. But Gerhardus got the better of the struggle. In the end he won. He fastened Karel to the wheel of his own wagon with the ox-riem. Then he thrashed him with the sjambok while Karel's wife and children were looking on.

That had happened years before. But nobody had forgotten. And now, in the Kalahari, when Gerhardus summoned us to a service, it was noticed that no man stayed away.

Just outside Malopolole is a muddy stream that is dry part of the year and part of the year has a foot or so of brackish water. We were lucky in being there just at the time when it had water. Early the following morning we filled up the water-barrels that we had put on our wagons before leaving the Marico. We were going right into the desert, and we did not know where we would get water again. Even the Bakwena kaffirs could not tell us for sure.

"The Great Dorstland Trek," Koos Steyn shouted as we got ready to move off. "Anyway, we won't fare as badly as the Dorstland Trekkers. We'll lose less cattle than they did because we've got less to lose. And seeing that we are only five families, not more than about a dozen of us will die of thirst."

I thought it was bad luck for Koos Steyn to make jokes like that about the Dorstland Trek, and I think that others felt the same way about it. We trekked right through that day, and it was all desert. By sunset we had not come across a sign of water anywhere. Abraham Ferreira said towards evening that perhaps it would be better if we went back to Malopolole and tried to find out for sure which was the best way of getting through the Kalahari. But the rest said that there was no need to do that, since we would be sure to come across water the next day. And, anyway, we were Doppers and, having once set out, we were not going to turn back. But after we had given the cattle water our barrels did not have too much left in them.

By the middle of the following day all our water had given out except a little that we kept for the children. But still we pushed on. Now that we had gone so far we were afraid to go back because of the long way that we would have to go without water to get back to Malopolole. In the evening we were very anxious. We all knelt down in the sand and prayed. Gerhardus Grobbelaar's voice sounded very deep and earnest when he besought God to have mercy on us, especially for the sakes of the little ones. He mentioned the baby Jemima by name. The Englishman knelt down beside me, and I noticed that he shivered when Gerhardus mentioned Koos Steyn's child.

It was moonlight. All around us was the desert. Our wagons seemed very small and lonely; there was something about them that looked very mournful. The women and children put their arms round one another and wept a long while. Our kaffirs stood some distance away and watched us. My wife Sannie put her hand in mine, and I thought of the concentration camp. Poor woman, she had suffered much. And I knew that her thoughts were the same as my own: that after all it was perhaps better that our children should have died then than now.

We had got so far into the desert that we began telling one another that we must be near the end. Although we knew that German West was far away, and that in the way we had been travelling we had got little more than into the beginning of the Kalahari, yet we tried to tell one another lies about how near water was likely to be. But, of course, we told those lies only to one another. Each man in his own heart knew what the real truth was. And later on we even stopped telling one another lies about what a good chance we had of getting out alive. You can understand how badly things had gone with us when you know that we no longer troubled about hiding our position from the women and children. They wept, some of them. But that made no difference then. Nobody tried to comfort the women and children who cried. We knew that tears were useless, and yet somehow at that hour we felt that the weeping of the women was not less useless than the courage of the men. After a while there was no more weeping in our camp. Some of the women who lived through the dreadful things of the days that came after, and got safely back to the Transvaal, never again wept. What they had seen appeared to have hardened them. In this respect they had become as men. I think that is the saddest thing that ever happens in this world, when women pass through great suffering that makes them become as men.

That night we hardly slept. Early the next morning the men went out to look for water. An hour after sun-up Ferreira came back and told us that he had found a muddy pool a few miles away. We all went there, but there wasn't much water. Still, we got a little, and that made us feel better. It was only when it came to driving our cattle towards the mudhole that we found our kaffirs had deserted us during the night. After we had gone to sleep they had stolen away. Some of the weaker cattle couldn't get up to go to the pool. So we left them. Some were trampled to death or got choked in the mud, and we had to pull them out to let the rest get to the hole. It was pitiful.

Just before we left one of Ferreira's daughters died. We scooped a hole in the sand and buried her.

So we decided to trek back.

After his daughter was dead Abraham Ferreira went up to Gerhardus and told him that if we had taken his advice earlier on and gone back, his daughter would not have died.

"Your daughter is dead now, Abraham," Gerhardus said. "It is no use talking about her any longer. We all have to die some day. I refused to go back earlier. I have decided to go back now."

Abraham Ferreira looked Gerhardus in the eyes and laughed. I shall always remember how that laughter sounded in the desert. In Abraham's voice there was the hoarseness of the sand and thirst. His voice was cracked with what the desert had done to him; his face was lined and his lips were blackened. But there was nothing about him that spoke of grief for his daughter's death.

"Your daughter is still alive, Oom Gerhardus," Abraham Ferreira said, pointing to the wagon wherein lay Gerhardus's wife, who was weak, and the child to whom she had given birth only a few months before. "Yes, she is still alive. . . so far."

Ferreira turned away laughing, and we heard him a little later explaining to his wife in cracked tones about the joke he had made.

Gerhardus Grobbelaar merely watched the other man walk away without saying anything. So far we had followed Gerhardus through all things, and our faith in him had been great. But now that we had decided to trek back we lost our belief in him. We lost it suddenly, too. We knew that it was best to turn back, and that to continue would mean that we would all die in the Kalahari. And yet, if Gerhardus had said we must still go on we would have done so. We would have gone through with him right to the end. But now that he as much as said he was beaten by the desert we had no more faith in Gerhardus. That is why I have said that Paul Kruger was a greater man than Gerhardus. Because Paul Kruger was that kind of man whom we still worshipped even when he decided to retreat. If it had been Paul Kruger who told us that we had to go back we would have returned with strong hearts. We would have retained exactly the same love for our leader, even if we knew that he was beaten. But from the moment that Gerhardus said we must go back we all knew that he was no longer our leader. Gerhardus knew that also.

We knew what lay between us and Malopolole and there was grave doubt in our hearts when we turned our wagons round. Our cattle were very weak, and we had to inspan all that could walk. We hadn't enough yokes, and therefore we cut poles from the scattered bushes and tied them to the trek-chains. As we were also without skeis we had to fasten the necks of the oxen straight on to the yokes with strops, and several of the oxen got strangled.

Then we saw that Koos Steyn had become mad. For he refused to return. He inspanned his oxen and got ready to trek on. His wife sat silent in the wagon with the baby; wherever her husband went she would go, too. That was only right, of course. Some women kissed her goodbye, and cried. But Koos Steyn's wife did not cry. We reasoned with Koos about it, but he said that he had made up his mind to cross the Kalahari, and he was not going to turn back just for nonsense.

"But, man," Gerhardus Grobbelaar said to him, "you've got no water to drink."

"I'll drink coffee then," Koos Steyn answered, laughing as always, and took up the whip and walked away beside the wagon. And Webber went off with him, just because Koos Steyn had been good to him, I suppose. That's why I have said that Englishmen are queer. Webber must have known that if Koos Steyn had not actually gone wrong in the head, still what he was doing now was madness, and yet he stayed with him.

We separated. Our wagons went slowly back to Malopolole. Koos Steyn's wagon went deeper into the desert. My wagon went last. I looked back at the Steyns. At that moment Webber also looked round. He saw me and waved his hand. It reminded me of that day in the Boer War when that other Englishman, whose companion we had shot, also turned round and waved.

Eventually we got back to Malopolole with two wagons and a handful of cattle. We abandoned the other wagons. Awful things happened on that desert. A number of children died. Gerhardus Grobbelaar's wagon was in front of me. Once I saw a bundle being dropped through the side of the wagon-tent. I knew what it was. Gerhardus would not trouble to bury his dead child, and his wife lay in the tent too weak to move. So I got off the wagon and scraped a small heap of sand over the body. All I remember of the rest of the journey to Malopolole is the sun and the sand. And the thirst. Although at one time we thought that we had lost our way, yet that did not matter much to us. We were past feeling. We could neither pray nor curse, our parched tongues cleaving to the roofs of our mouths.

Until today I am not sure how many days we were on our way back, unless I sit down and work it all out, and then I suppose I get it wrong. We got back to Malopolole and water. We said we would never go away from there again. I don't think that even those parents who had lost children grieved about them then. They were stunned with what they had gone through. But I knew that later on it would all come back again. Then they would remember things about shallow graves in the sand, and Gerhardus Grobbelaar and his wife would think of a little bundle lying out in the Kalahari. And I knew how they would feel.

Afterwards we fitted out a wagon with fresh oxen; we took an abundant supply of water and went back into the desert to look for the Steyn family. With the help of the Sechuana kaffirs, who could see tracks that we could not see, we found the wagon. The oxen had been outspanned;

a few lay dead beside the wagon. The kaffirs pointed out to us footprints on the sand, which showed which way those two men and that woman had gone.

In the end we found them.

Koos Steyn and his wife lay side by side in the sand; the woman's head rested on the man's shoulder; her long hair had become loosened, and blew about softly in the wind. A great deal of fine sand had drifted over their bodies. Near them the Englishman lay, face downwards. We never found the baby Jemima. She must have died somewhere along the way and Koos Steyn must have buried her. But we agreed that the Englishman Webber must have passed through terrible things; he could not even have had any understanding left as to what the Steyns had done with their baby. He probably thought, up to the moment when he died, that he was carrying the child. For, when we lifted his body, we found, still clasped in his dead and rigid arms, a few old rags and a child's clothes.

It seemed to us that the wind that always stirs in the Kalahari blew very quietly and softly that morning.

Yes, the wind blew very gently.

A BOER RIP VAN WINKEL

Every writer has got, lying around somewhere in a suitcase or a trunk, various parts of a story that he has worked on from time to time and that he has never finished, because he hasn't been able to find out how the theme should be handled. Such a story – that I have had lying in a suitcase for many years – centres around the things that happened to Herklaas van Wyk.

The plot of a story has no particular appeal for me. I feel that to sit down and work out a plot does not call for the highest form of literary inspiration. Rather does that form of activity recall the skill of the inventor.

My own stories that I like best are those that have just grown. Some mood, conjured up in half a dozen words, has set me going, and it has often happened to me that only when I have got to very near the end in the writing of it, has the shape of the story suddenly dawned on me. And more than once I have been surprised to find what a very old tale it was that has kept me from the chimney corner. Agreeably surprised, that is, for I have a preference for old tales.

But my inability to finish writing the story of Herklaas van Wyk is not due to the denouement not having taken some recognisable form in my mind within the last few hundred words. It hasn't been that kind of writer's problem: I didn't put my hand in the hat and a story came out that wouldn't unfold. On the contrary, this story told itself quite all right, in all its main essentials. What is more, within the first few paragraphs I realised very clearly to what general class of story it belonged. But there were so many hiatuses between the time when Herklaas van Wyk was last seen with the remnants of the Losberg commando, towards the end of the Boer War, in 1902, and the time when he was captured with General Kemp outside Upington in the rebellion of 1914.

If I could fill in that interval of a dozen years satisfactorily, I would still be able to write the story of Herklaas van Wyk. Yet the very fascination of this story is intimately bound up with the *nature* of that lacuna. It is no new thing to have a story of which the end is a mystery – something that the reader must work out for himself with or without a clue supplied by the author. But when the middle part of a story – which gives the atmosphere to the whole sequence of real and imaginary events – is missing, then I feel that I am confronted with an artistic problem of an order that I am not sure it is wise for a writer to tackle.

I don't mind writing a story in which the plot is vague. But when the atmosphere isn't there – the background and the psychology and the interplay of situation and character – then what is left isn't my idea of a story.

The events with which Herklaas van Wyk was connected in the early part of 1902 were commonplace enough. There are still a number of Boers alive today who were on commando with him. Kritzinger's invasion of the Cape Colony is an episode that has passed into history. And a considerable body of Boers, members of commandos that kept being split up into ever-smaller groups, succeeded in penetrating to the Atlantic Ocean and in remaining in the field, deep inside the Cape Colony, long after the main commando had retreated beyond the Vaal.

It was in 1902 that Herklaas van Wyk, then promoted to the rank of veldkornet, caught sight, in the blue distance, of the unquiet Atlantic. The small body of men pushed on to the beach. They had come a long way, from the Transvaal and the Free State, and also from the Karoo, where a number of Cape rebels had joined the fighting forces of the Republics. It was a mixed group of burghers that came to a halt on the white sand of the beach south of Okiep.

Herklaas van Wyk rode his horse along the shore for a considerable distance. The burghers galloped on behind their veldkornet, the hooves of their horses kicking up a spray of damp sea-sand. For they rode along that strip of beach from which the waves had withdrawn in the ebbing of the Atlantic.

Eventually Herklaas van Wyk reined in his horse. His hand shielding his eyes, he gazed for a long while at the place where the sea and sky met on the horizon. He had known two years before that the Boer War was lost for the Transvaal and the Free State. One last hope had returned to him, early that morning, when he had caught sight of the ocean. That hope, too, had vanished now. He realised that he would not be able, with the handful of burghers under his command, to invade England.

Facing out to the sea, Herklaas van Wyk slowly took off his hat.

"It's no good, kêrels," he called out above the roar of the waves and the wind, "we'll have to get back again. There's no drift around here where we'll be able to get our horses through."

About Herklaas van Wyk there was a certain measure of grandeur even in defeat.

And his story, up to that time when the sea-wind was whistling through his black beard, was straightforward enough. In fact, you can read about him in any history book dealing with that period. But it is on his way back to the Transvaal, when he and his men had to elude flying English columns and had to cross barbed-wire fences with blockhouses threaded on to them, that Herklaas van Wyk quits the pages of printed history, complete with dates and place-names, and enters the realm of legend.

It is generally accepted that he was still in the field when the Boer War ended in May, 1902. His own story is that he crept into a deserted rondavel at the foot of a koppie in the Upington District, and that he fell asleep there, with his Mauser beside him, and his horse tethered to a thorn-tree.

Another story – subscribed to on doubtful authority by fellow members of the rebel commando that surrendered with Herklaas van Wyk in 1915, after General Kemp had failed to take Upington – seeks to account for that interval of a dozen years in a different fashion. In terms of this latter attempt at reconstructing the facts, all that happened to Herklaas van Wyk between 1902, the end of the Boer War, and 1914, the year of the outbreak of the rebellion, was that he lived on some farm in the Upington District as a bywoner. It is readily conceivable, protagonists of this standpoint declare, that he slept quite a lot during that period, especially on hot afternoons when his employer had sent him out to look for strayed cattle. Who has not heard – this school of the doubters asks – of a bywoner lying asleep in his rondavel when he should be at the borehole pumping water?

I can only reply that this theory which represents him as a decadent bywoner does not fit in with my conception of Herklaas van Wyk as a person.

A third school of theorists, drawing attention to the scar of an old bullet wound that Herklaas van Wyk still carried above his left temple when he rode with Kemp in 1915, offers another explanation of that interim period. Quite likely that bullet, searing the flesh at the side of his head, caused loss of memory, they say. Quite likely Herklaas van Wyk did become a bywoner when the Boer War ended. And then, in 1914, when he again heard the hoofbeats of commandos coming out of the veld, and the rattling of musketry, the past was suddenly brought back to him, and he was once more in the saddle, with his Mauser and bandolier. The Boer War came back to him in a single rush. Only, the bywoner period now sank into oblivion. Memory does play tricks like that.

Well, I must confess that I don't care particularly for this latter theory, either.

I still prefer Herklaas van Wyk's own story, which he told to anybody who would listen, after he had been captured by Botha's Government forces. For one thing, if we accept Herklaas van Wyk's account of his long sleep in the abandoned rondavel at the foot of a koppie in the Upington District, we have the material for a South African legend as stirring as the one that Washington Irving chronicled. Van Wyk and Van Winkel. This is surely no idle coincidence. Above all, there is a Gothic quality in Herklaas van Wyk's own story – a gloomy magnificence that is never absent from the interior of a rondavel at the foot of a koppie, if that koppie is composed of ironstone.

Herklaas van Wyk asleep in a dark corner, waiting, a backveld Barbarossa, for his far-off awakening, in an hour filled with the thunder of horse-hooves and the noise of battle.

The old man with the white beard and the rusty Mauser and the walking skeleton of a horse had been with Kemp's rebel commando for the best part of a week of dispirited running away from the Government forces. It now began to dawn on the little band of 1914 rebels that Oom Herklaas van Wyk was (as they interpreted it) in his second childhood. It was clear that he thought the year was 1902; it was obvious that he did not know that he was a rebel who had taken the field against the Union troops; instead, he spoke of himself as a Transvaal burgher, and he referred to Cronje's surrender at Paardeberg, scornfully, as though it had taken place yesterday.

He was very puzzled, also, when he learnt for the first time that the rebel commando was being pursued by a column of Botha-men.

"But if Botha is chasing us," Herklaas van Wyk demanded, "who is fighting Kitchener?"

Thus it came about, one evening when the rebels were encamped in a blue-gum plantation on the road to Upington, that a lot of explanations were made.

"I remember the day you joined us, Oom Herklaas," Jan Gouws, a young rebel, said after Herklaas van Wyk had told his story and they had persuaded him that the year was, indeed, 1915, and that he was not now fighting in the Boer War. "Your white beard was blowing in the wind, Oom Herklaas, and several of us laughed at the awkward way your old horse cantered, throwing his legs all to one side. So you really say you slept for twelve years?"

"I believe now – now that you've told me," Herklaas van Wyk replied, "that I must have lain asleep on the floor of that rondavel all those years. That must have been just at the end of the Boer War. And it's funny that I didn't wake up before my nation again needed me."

The rebels received the old man's last remark in silence. They were beginning to doubt the wisdom of their armed rising. They had been driven from pillar to post for many days. Incessant rain had damped their ardour.

"Did you remember to wind your watch before you went to sleep in that rondavel, Oom Herklaas?" Jan Gouws asked, trying to change the subject.

The others did not laugh at this sally. For one thing, the rain had started coming down again. . .

Some of the rebels seemed half-inclined to believe Herklaas van Wyk's story. And there seemed to be something inexplicably solemn in the thought of a burgher of the Transvaal Republic going to sleep in the corner of a deserted rondavel, with his Mauser at his side – and only waking up again a dozen years later, when men were once more riding with rifles slung across their shoulders.

"Did you dream at all during that time, Oom Herklaas?" another man asked, in a half-serious tone.

The old man thought for a little while.

"I remember dreaming about a mossie settling on a kaffir-boom that was full of red flowers," Herklaas van Wyk answered slowly, "but I think I dreamt of it a long time back – after I had been asleep only four years, or so."

Jan Gouws shivered. The red flowers on that kaffir-boom must be pretty well faded by now, he thought. And it gave him a queer feeling to think of that mossie, that an old man saw in a dream, flitting about in the sunshine of long ago. It made Jan Gouws feel uncomfortable, for a reason that he could not explain.

"My Mauser is very rusty," Herklaas van Wyk continued. "I've tried oiling it, but that doesn't help. I'll have to hands-up or shoot one of the enemy, and take his Lee-Metford off him, like we used to do. How long will it take us to win this war, do you think?"

The rebels did not answer. They knew that their cause was already shot to pieces. In spite of the old man's senility, there seemed to emanate from his spirit a strange kind of assurance, a form of steadfastness in the face of adversity and defeat that they themselves did not possess. It seemed that there was something inside the entrails of this burgher of the Transvaal Republic that they didn't have. Something firm and constant that they had lost. And they felt, sensing the difference between the previous generation and their own, and without being able to express their feelings in words, that in that difference lay their defeat.

"What happened about your horse, Oom Herklaas?" a young rebel asked eventually.

Outwardly dilapidated, Herklaas van Wyk still seemed to represent, somehow, the gloom and grandeur of a greater day.

"I had tethered my horse to a thorn-tree," Herklaas van Wyk said, "and he, too, must have fallen asleep. And I am sure that the hoofbeats of a commando at full gallop must have awakened him, also. For when I got to the thorn-tree – which hadn't grown much during that time: you know how slowly a thorn-tree grows – my old war-horse was sniffing the wind and pawing the ground. And his neck was arched."